The Mango Tree

Stories & Sketches

For Steele
love
Sally May
4 . 5 . 2015

Anthea Senaratna

ISBN: 978-955-97754-1-6

First Edition - January, 2008
Second Edition - February, 2011
Third Edition - October, 2013

Cover Illustration
Anthea Senaratna

Graphics
Charithanga Vithanage

Printers
Ari Investments Private Ltd., Nugegoda
2852410, 2820019
ariyaw@gmail.com

II

Contents

Foreword

I am happy to be asked to write this foreword for Anthea's new book of short stories.

What I like best about her stories is her understanding of people. She does not need to describe her characters feature by feature. They present themselves so crystal clear by their speech and actions that we can see them, hear them, visualize the circumstances in which they have their being and feel the particular strengths and weaknesses of each individual.

Internecine war has changed people and these are some of the people Anthea describes in her book. She makes no judgments but leaves it to the reader to form his or her own opinion. There is no overwriting; her stories are compact and leave one thinking, "Do we not also know these people?"

Behind Anthea's enormous sympathy and understanding there is also wisdom that lets her stand back and assess, sometimes with a glint of humour, always with affection.

I have enjoyed reading these stories and wish this book the success it deserves.

Christine Wilson
Colombo
2006

Two Pieces of Chicken

I was just about to leave when I heard the lady shout.
"Manika! Tell that girl to wait."
I worked twice a week at this house. Manika was the permanent maid, but I went every Monday and Thursday to sweep the garden and do the house work. Manika did only the cooking now as her arthritis made it difficult for her to do all the work.

It was a small but comfortable house. I wished so much I could live in a house like that. When I thought of my own house, with its leaky tin roof and broken doors and windows I felt sick.

My husband ran away with some woman many years ago, so now I had to work and look after my children. Ramani at thirteen was just beginning to fill out and Dinuk was a skinny nine year old. They attended the government school so I didn't have to pay fees, but clothing and feeding them cost me every cent I earned.

Each time I arranged the beds in this house I let my fingers feel the soft clean sheets and plump pillows. Even the bathrooms smelt nice. There was a plastic bottle with some scented water which I had to spray all over the two bathrooms after I had cleaned them. They smelt like flowers. The kitchen was bright and airy and spotless. The plates shone, the glasses shone, and I could see my reflection in the gleaming saucepans. The lady was very kind to me. She often gave me titbits of food and even bought me packets of noodles and other things which I could not afford. There were two dogs in the house. They ate all the expensive foods. Chicken and liver and beef. I wished my children could eat like that sometimes. I was allowed to serve myself lunch and often I would keep part of it to take home for my children.

The lady came into Manika's kitchen. She was tall and thin and wore baggy long dresses in the house. Her fair face became red when she was excited or angry. Now it was red because she was angry. Manika stared at me keeping her eyes off the blue plastic bag I carried everywhere with me.

"Manika, I kept two pieces of chicken in the 'fridge to use for the soup tonight - now they're missing - are they here?"

Manika looked into the saucepans and peered at the plates as if the two pieces would suddenly appear in one of them.

I clutched onto the blue bag trying to look unconcerned about this hullabaloo.

"Missy can I go now - I have finished all my work."

"Finished? Finished - you are not to leave- come here."

As I stepped forward she grabbed the bag from me and upset its contents onto the kitchen counter. My dirty handkerchief and small *malla* with my money fell out. Then a plastic container - an old Flora Margarine box, tumbled out. The lady pulled it open and there lay the two pieces of chicken. Fleshy juicy pieces, covered in a dark gravy which tasted like the best curry I had ever eaten. I wanted to run away - to pretend I had nothing to do with all that, but my feet were heavy and stuck to the ground. I could hardly breathe.

"Hah - what is this - hah? How did this get into your bag? Did these two pieces walk into your bag?" She shook my shoulder. I choked and tears streamed down my face.

"Manika- did you know about this, hah?"she screamed.

There was no point in my saying that Manika had given me the chicken.

"As though I will give her chicken." Manika looked at me, her eyes glaring at my foolishness at getting caught.

The lady put my day's wage onto the counter, "There take your money and go - don't come back." Her lips trembled as she spoke. She turned and went inside.

I picked up the money and took my handkerchief and *mallu* from the counter and put them into the blue bag. Manika disappeared into her room. I stepped over the sleeping dog and walked to the gate. I didn't really mean to steal it at all - I just thought, well two pieces of chicken curry, how my children would love to eat that! I was going to make some *roti* to eat with this - and maybe even make a little *lunu miris*- it was going to be such a treat for us. Even Manika agreed with me at the time. "You can take this back with you - no one will want this here," she said putting it into the old Flora Margarine container. But now, we had nothing. No chicken, no treat and I had lost my job in the best house I worked in. The other places never allowed me to even serve my food. Their 'fridges were locked, the cupboards locked, they never gave me anything extra and made me work really hard. I wished the lady had slapped me or hit me - at least I would have felt that I had paid for my wrongdoing. But now she just told me not to come back. My mouth felt sour and dry, for without this job what was I going to do?

I stopped at the corner of the road and looked back at the house. At least for a few hours every week I enjoyed the comforts of a lifestyle I could never afford. Now two pieces of chicken had lost everything for me. How I hated that chicken. I hated Manika and the lady and those fat dogs they had. I hated my children at that moment for it was for them I had taken the chicken. If they had not been there I would never have done it.

I stopped at the *kade* to buy some bread and a coconut. We'll have to eat just *sambol* and bread tonight.

3

The children were playing in the compound which served all the tenements there.

"Ah *amma, amma!*" they cried when they saw me, "*Amma* what have you got in the blue bag today? Did the lady give anything for us?" They followed me into the house. I pushed them aside and they stopped laughing and shouting. I threw the bag at them.

"There look inside - that's all I have." I burst into tears and shouted at them. "Because of you I took - no I stole two pieces of chicken. I did it for you and now I have no job." The sobs came gushing out. I went into our small wooden shack and pulled out my mat which was rolled up in the corner. I lay down and closed my eyes.

After some time I looked up. Everything was quiet. The glow of an oil lamp shed a dim light in the corner. The children sat huddled in the doorway biting their nails, their big eyes staring at me.

They came running to me when they saw that I was awake. "Doesn't matter *amma,* we'll eat the bread and I'll scrape the coconut for some *sambol.* You must be tired."

Dinuk took so long to scrape the coconut. His small thin hands went on and on and on and yet there was just a handful in the plate. Ramani was cutting the bread, large lopsized chunks.

What am I doing to them, I thought. Punishing them for my sins.

I stood up and took the bottle of chillie pieces and squeezed the last quarter of lime in the house.

"Let's make a *sambol*." I said, trying to smile.

I waited for two whole weeks before I could gather enough courage to go back to the house. I couldn't find any replacement work. So now I had only two days of work each week which was not at all enough for us to live on. I had to try to get my job back. Ramani asked whether she and

4

Dinuk could go and beg from the lady, but I didn't want to put them through all this. It was my fault after all, so I had to deal with it.

I dug out some savings from the money I hid in my pillow and put this in my *malla*. My heart thudded hard against my chest. I set out for the house. First I went to the *kade* at the top of their road, looking out to see whether I could meet Manika when she came there to buy the bread. I waited for some minutes but didn't see her.

I felt the weight of the money in my *malla*. Two hundred and eighty rupees - a huge amount for me.

What if my plan didn't work, I thought? But it was my only chance.

"I want to buy a chicken." I told the *mudalali* at the *kade*. "A big one."

He raised his eyebrows, for never had I bought anything so expensive from him.

"Ah, you're having a party hah?" he smirked.

My clammy fingers moved slowly as I counted the mass of coins. He went through the money carefully before he handed the chicken over to me. He always tried to save on the plastic bags and the one he gave me just fitted over the chicken. My fingers could hardly get the loops together to carry it.

The iced chicken made my hand numb. I walked slowly towards the house. The bright red gate which was such a warming sight before, now looked strange and forbidding. I stood outside for many minutes. Then I peered over. The dogs rushed out, barking and wagging their stumpy tails in greeting. Manika came out.

"Ah Mala - how -?" she looked over the gate and spoke softly. "*Aiyo* Mala I miss you.." She paused. "Have you found another job?"

"No Manika" I looked down.

"Must be hard for you no?"

5

"Has - has missy got someone else?" My mouth tasted bitter.

"No - she does the work now."

My hand was becoming frozen. "Manika - I have brought a present - a chicken for the lady. I thought if I returned a chicken I could get my job back."

"The lady is having a bath - you will have to wait till she finishes."

I waited in the shade of the little tree with the pink flowers outside the gate. This was the tree which the parrots visited. How I loved to watch them as they picked the seeds from the pods which hung on its branches. I shifted the chicken from hand to hand as the ice began to make my hands all wet. After many minutes Manika appeared and took the chicken. I could hear them talking inside.

How I longed to be there, seated on the small *bankuwa* against the kitchen door, sipping my hot tea, listening to the sounds of the radio. I could picture the lady seated at the small table looking up from the newspaper as Manika walked in. I heard their voices but not their words.

After what seemed ages, Manika came out with the chicken in her hand.

"Mala, the lady says she does not want the chicken, she says for you to take it back home - *Aiyo* this is all melting no." she said, as she gave it to me over the gate. The chicken had begun to thaw and the whole bag was becoming wet now. I held it from the top and began walking back home. It was so heavy. My chest hurt and my eyes blurred.

I bit my lip and tried hard not to let the tears come down. No no, I won't show them how desperate I am. I'll cook the chicken for us to eat. We can have a feast. Paupers' feast. That sounded funny.

I heard all sorts of sounds- clapping, shouting. Maybe the neighbours were all laughing at me trying to get my job back after stealing some chicken. The shouting suddenly became louder.

"Mala, Mala." It was Manika, running up to me. She was panting as she caught my shoulder. I stood still.

"Mala- *aiyo* I am so tired by running – Mala you went off before I could finish telling you that the lady said to come back to work - come tomorrow." She gave me her toothless grin. I just stood, dazed. My throat felt all funny and choked. It didn't bother me that the chicken dripped and that my fingers were near frozen as I walked back home.

Aftermath

The war had been over for nearly seven months now. Mahen still awoke at 5.00 am, as he did when he was in the army. The low-ceilingd room was gloomy and the closed windows made it hot and stuffy. But he could hear bird song outside his window. That was the best part of living out of Colombo, for the large garden that surrounded their house was a haven to a number of birds. It took him back to his schooldays when he roamed the fields nearby. The song was chirpy, signifying perhaps the bliss that had settled upon the country. Peace, at last. This is what the people longed for - sick and tired of a war that eroded every part of the land for over twenty years. Now at last, they could live without the threat of bombs and killings, without the hassle of checkpoints that dotted the country, without the need for identity cards to be carried on them at all times. Now at last, with the shackles of war discarded, this island could move forward to meeting its match with its progressive neighbours.

But the quietness of the morning didn't soothe him, instead it made him restless, wanting to get up and do something; but what? He lay in bed and recalled yesterday – when his aunt and uncle and cousins from Colombo visited. They had walked in talking loud and laughing, but the minute he stepped out of his room they'd just stopped and stared at him, looking at one another uneasily, not knowing quite what to say or do. Embarrassed? Ashamed? He'd never know.

"Ah! *Putha!* " his uncle had finally forced the words out of his throat, "how nice to see you again. You must be so happy that the war is over and you can settle down at last."

He remained silent. How can I 'settle' down to a life I've not known for so many years? I had work to do every single day I was in the army, but now I dread each new day, the unknown day that will bear down on me.

The day it happened -the day his face was injured – was permanently etched in his memory. How else could it be? There he was, gun in hand firing away when all of a sudden, a sound like thunder, a flash of lightning, and he was hurled into nowhere. All he felt was a thud on his back and a razor-sharp stinging on his face. His own screams pierced his head and then he blacked out. The weeks and weeks of having a bandage round his eyes, lying in a hospital bed, and how when they took it off he screamed in despair as he couldn't see anything at all. But then suddenly he woke up early one morning, like this very morning, and was aware of a dim light filtering into the ward. Everything was still and quiet and only the sound of breathing could be heard. He sat up on his bed and rummaged through the drawer on the side table for the small mirror he had there. But when he looked into it he couldn't believe that this raw looking hideous thing in the reflection was his face. He couldn't even cry for his tear ducts were still not functioning after the operation. I just want to die, I just want to die, he kept thinking. Then, as if to relieve the monotonous gloom he heard a bird sing – like a tinkle of glass bells. The magpie robin was serenading the new day.

Living with a half blown off face was the hardest thing for him. Everyone said how lucky he was to be alive, but as he gazed at his face in the mirror and his half closed eyes lingered on the mutilated nose and mouth, he felt that this was the worst thing that could have happened to him. To anyone. People looked at your face when they spoke to you, but in his case, they looked away, like they were talking to someone by his side, some invisible being. At least with a missing hand or leg they could still look you in the eye, but with a disfigured face with one eye almost completely closed and the other set at an angle and his cheek drawn taut on that side, where were they to look?

He got up silently, through habit, so as not to awaken anyone. He remembered the number of places he had slept in. Under the stars, under heavy canopied tents, under trees, in dormitories – so many places where he had rested his weary body. He trembled when he thought of the bunkers – they were the worst – closed in and stifling, choking the air out of him. A cynical laugh escaped his lips, when he even tried to imagine any of his friends or family sleeping in such circumstances. But he, Mahen, now thirty-four, he who had been in the army ever since he was twenty two, he could sleep anywhere.

Right this minute I need a cigarette. He felt around for the packet on his bedside table. The matches lit and then died and his hand shook as he struck one then another and another. Bloody hell! I need a drink then – I need something to ease this emptiness.

His mother had insisted he use a wardrobe, engraved on either side with flowers and silver handles on the doors, for the clothes she'd bought him. After the rough feel of army fatigues against his body and heavy boots on his feet, the shirts and trousers and sandals he had to wear now gave him a strange sensation, almost like being someone else. He had returned home to recuperate, by which time the peace process was almost completed, and hardly ever ventured out of the house. While at home he decided to stick to what was comfortable for him, so he wore a sarong,

10

tied with a knot around his waist; the loose flowing cloth keeping him cool against the scorching heat at this time of the year.

Reaching out into the back of the shelf, his fingers felt the long neck and gentle curve of the bottle he had tucked away under some clothes. They'd make a bloody fuss if they came across it, he thought. He always locked his wardrobe. He sneered at the word; it was just a cupboard, but they loved to use posh words like that, made them happy and comfortable. The key hung safely round his neck so no one could get at it. They'd become snoopy over the months after he'd returned. He was sure his mother, or his sister who had grown old and wizened since her husband died, used to rummage through his things out of curiosity, maybe in the hope of discovering some secret about him.

He put the bottle to his mouth and took a deep swig, the liquid stung his throat, burning down his gullet as it flowed into his stomach. Three of those, and a kind of lightness settled on him. It felt like walking on air and he felt ready to do something, anything. He just wanted to get away from this room; stifling, like being inside a bunker.

I wish I could have my gun again; my beloved gun, my constant companion, such perfect lines, the cold touch of steel. Where the hell was it? Rushing to his bed he pulled aside sheets, threw pillows on the floor. He peered under the bed, then he remembered, they'd taken it away from him when this damn peace thing came about. How could they have done that to him after all he did for them, for his country? They made such a big speech at his farewell. But for him there was no peace. He collapsed on his bed, curled on his side and hugged his pillow between his legs. All these years I seldom had even one pillow and now I have

11

two. Lucky me, he thought, tasting the saltiness of his tears.

Now he heard familiar voices, the house was waking up to attend to the many tasks of the coming day. His mother's voice floated like bird song, gentle and soothing. He felt drowsy and closed his eyes.

When he awoke his mother's face was hovering over him. She broke into a smile and bent down to sit on his bed.
"Come, get up *Putha*, you can have your breakfast. But first have a wash, there's soap and everything in the bathroom. Then tell me what you want. I'm making your favourite *pittu, rotti and lunumiris*." She touched his head. What would she say if she knew I'd already had a nice long drink? That would shock her – my old mother. I shouldn't do this, she loves me so much, but I hate it when she looks at me like this. All of them do- they force smiles which mask their pity and sympathy. My God I can't bear it!
"I'll come," he said, and she left the room.

He closed his eyes. What the hell am I going to do today? Twenty-four bloody hours, how many minutes, how many seconds? An eternity. I'll nap in the afternoon at least four hours, then go to sleep at least eight hours – that still leaves twelve hours. To do what? No operations to go on, no planning to do, never again will I feel the excitement of firing a shot and getting the enemy. Oh the time I was surprised by one of those bastards trying to creep into the camp, how I got hold of him and twisted his neck. I'll never forget the look on his face and the way his eyeballs almost jumped out of their sockets. How he tried to scream but only a little croak came out of his throat and then he stopped. So easy to kill a man just with one twist. like wringing out the washing. I always obeyed orders – don't

12

spare the enemy – kill the bastards off- every single one of them. Never again will I have my colleague, my comrades, my dearest brothers, they're all gone anyhow, or most of them. Only Sunil and some others were left. Many of them were either paralyzed or limbless. But I, Mahen, had been singled out by Fate and was the only one who kept my body and limbs intact and got my face blasted.

"Putha," his mother was calling him again.
I'll have to get up and go to the table even if it's just to please her. He adjusted his sarong and put on a banian before he left the room. They had told him over and over again to come 'dressed' to the table. Not to come bare chested.
The dining room was a din of noise. The high pitched voices of children's chatter hurt his ears and the adults were talking and laughing loud. But everything stopped when he walked in The voices stopped, the laughter stopped, the movements stopped, only the ticking of the clock could be heard.
"Putha come and sit here." His mother pulled the chair back and held him as he sat. The children were staring at him. His father looked old and feeble as he sat at the head of the table not saying a word. A wordless head he thought, laughing within. *Thaththa* never did speak much, even when we were kids, he just went to work and came back and *Amma* did all the talking. But now, they were all silent, staring. Every day for the past so many months this is how he was greeted. Weren't they ever going to get used to his face? But how could they when even I am not used to it? The painful silence hung like a thundercloud weighing down on him until he almost screamed. He looked down at his plate not wanting to meet their inquisitive eyes.

Eyes. Like the glistening eyes in the black faces which stared from behind the huts as my comrades and I walked through the village. Kill them all, we were ordered, don't let even one survive. I lifted my gun and fired – and how they dropped, one by one, like mangoes off a tree – plop plop plop. Then - it was too much, too much- I couldn't go on - I fell down. Someone pulled me up. Get moving, get moving, they shouted. We moved. We walked over dead bodies- strewn all over. The smell of burning was awful – all those houses and all those bodies charred. The entire village wiped out. Razed to the ground.

The smell of burning hit his nostrils.
"There's something burning!" he cried, springing up from his chair.
"No *Putha* it's only the *rotti* I'm making," it was his mother speaking as she put two small *rottis* on his plate.
She made the *rotti* on a flat griddle over the fire on the cooker.
"Here, take your fried egg I've already put some salt and pepper on it. And some fish curry – you always liked *rotti* with egg and fish curry. Manika has made some good *lunumiris* – have some."
"Pass him the *rotti*," his sister's voice.
His sister's children stood by the table. The girl child stared at him while she got her books into a back-pack and slung it over her shoulders. The boy was younger – maybe about ten. He was mumbling as he cast furtive glances towards him. Must be saying what a horror I look.

I wonder what happened to my own backpack? Oh my backpack, such a part of me! How it clung to my body making me look like a hunchback. How we laughed and shouted in protest when we had to lug the seventeen kilos we were trained to carry in it, and moaned in agony when

14

we all ended up with bad necks. That damned dreadful hot collar I sometimes had to wear when the pain got really bad. Where's my backpack now – wonder whether they threw it away? Like I've been thrown away. He grimaced. They took everything away except the old uniforms and the medal.

"*Amma*, I want the uniforms."
"Eat your breakfast *putha.*"
"What about the uniforms? My uniforms." He jabbed the egg with a piece of rotti and the yellow ran loose on his plate.
"They're at the laundry."
"Still?"
"Yes – now eat your breakfast."

Silence.
"Where's my medal then?"
"I've kept it in a safe place?"
"Yes, but *where?* It's mine, I want it now." He beat his fist on the table, making the plates jump.
His mother stared at him and walked away.
The children muttered and his sister spoke to them in hushed tones.
Then he saw the gleaming thing in the box his mother held out to him.
"Here." She put it on the table.
His hand shook as he felt the cold metal strike his fingers. This was when I was promoted and became a Major- after the attack on the terrorist camp up North- and before my face – before it happened. We fired mortar after mortar and it took a good forty minutes to kill the buggers off. Afterwards, when we walked through we found their bodies – pieces of flesh, body parts -a hand here, a foot there and even a head thrown somewhere in the bushes. So bloody

weird. Dead heads with their eyes opened wide. My god what a sight! What a bloody weird sight!

There was a stinging silence at the dining table.
Then his sister spoke. "You two better hurry up or you'll miss the bus." The children left quietly for school, backpacks full of books and God knows what – heavy as hell, making their shoulders droop.

After they'd gone, his sister went off to her teaching job, mumbling as she left. His mother gathered the plates from the table and took them to Manika who had already begun washing up at the kitchen sink.
He ate slowly and looked across at his father who was nursing a cup of tea. His father spoke to him looking out into space at some non-existent being, some invisible thing out there. Why did he do this, every single time? Is my face so horrible-that my own father cannot look at me when he speaks to me?
"What about a job *Putha*? "
"What job?"
"Soma Uncle said there's a vacancy in the Ceramics Corporation – might be able to fit you in."
He didn't reply. They'll really have to 'fit' me in- he smirked to himself.
He recalled the last job interview – they had stared so much at him at the Reception desk that he had just turned around, jumped into the first three-wheeler and gone straight back home. He had never felt so out of place, like a freak on show. After the accident, while he was in hospital he never felt like this. For he was among his own kind, all equally exposed to the cruel ravages of war. His pain was their pain, his suffering theirs. Fates bonded in brotherhood.

He spent the day listening to the radio, reading the newspapers, and falling asleep in between. The news was full of the peace proceedings, peace plans, peace everything. End of war- now it's happy time- happy days are here again. Everything's going to be wonderful from now on. He turned the radio on to the music channel and kept it on while he had his lunch. The songs blared out and he soon tired of the bubbly sounds. He lay on his bed and slept till evening.

Evening. Mahen always welcomed this time of the day. The quiet onset of dusk, when everything looked hazy and dim. He went out to the verandah and lay back on the *haansi puttuwa* in the corner. A cool breeze wafted through the trees. He closed his eyes and wished he were back in his childhood, when things were uncomplicated and simple. Schooldays, friends -and girls and teasing. Girls – I wonder what happened to them? All those sisters of the boys in school whom we used to eye with such longing? And laughter- we laughed so much those days – at what? I can't even remember. At nothing perhaps. Or at everything.

The click of the gate latch made him sit up with a start. He leaned forward clutching his sarong, ready to dash inside. Then he relaxed, for through the soft veil of light he recognized his neighbour and friend Sugath.

Sugath looked so good. Tall, handsome- his face a chiseled piece of sculpture- sharp nose, set mouth, bright eyes under dark eyebrows, a strong firm chin. The kind of face I used to have. In school, we were so alike we were often mistaken for brothers. But now everything had changed.

"How *machang*?" Sugath greeted Mahen in his usual buoyant manner looking directly at him.

"I got back from Singapore last night. Here, I brought these for you." He thrust a large plastic bag on Mahen's lap.

"So, how was your training programme?" Mahen asked.

"Good men - quite hectic." Sugath sat. "So *machang* what have you been doing?"

"Nothing much. Nothing really." He paused. "Actually, I haven't being doing a damn thing, what the hell can I do anyway?"

Silence.

"You don't like to get a job *machang*?"

"Job? What kind of job can I get – looking – looking like this?" He touched his face.

"Don't be silly, no one is going to be bothered about your face – after all a job is a job. You can easily get something with your flair for maths. You did your CIMA didn't you?"

"Yes – but that was so long ago Sugath. I never got any experience in accountancy after I joined the army."

"There's a vacancy in our office for an assistant accountant. Why don't you apply? I'll help you."

Mahen fidgeted with the hem of his banian. He pulled at the loose threads.

"Why don't we write out an application? I can get *nangi* to do it nicely on her computer."

Sugath went into the house and came out with a sheet of paper and pen. He took a magazine from the rack by his chair and placed it on his knee.

" Okay- now tell me your qualifications and experience then I can do it."

"What qualifications?"

"Why men, your army experience and all that?"

"Army experience? Just obeying orders *machang* – that's all it was. They say jump and you jump, kill and you kill – simple." He held up his hands and held an invisible gun. "Da-da-da-da-da – there -the buggers are all dead. Shot by me, Major Mahen Wimalasuriya."

Sugath stood up. "I know it's hard *machang*, but you have to be positive. He reached out and touched Mahen's shoulder. I'll be back soon."

It'll be so strange for me to go to an office every day instead of to the field. They must be having really posh offices now. They'll all be smartly dressed and I'll just have the clothes *amma* got for me – can't remember when I last bought myself any clothes. I can see them all staring at me and laughing behind my back – that weird army guy without a face, they'll say.

A while later Sugath returned with a neat word-processed application.

Mahen read it slowly. "I don't know about this Sugath."

"Just sign it – I'll do everything I can to get you in- you'll see."

With a sigh Mahen reached out and signed the letter.

As he rose to go back to his room Mahen saw the plastic bag on the floor by his chair. He peered inside and his fingers fumbled as he unwrapped a white cotton shirt, a pair of grey slacks, and a blue tie. His eyes blurred, for it was a long time since he had bought himself anything and even longer since anyone had given him a present. Sugath, my dearest friend.

A week passed by. He must've told them about me and they must have thrown my application in the basket. But to his surprise one evening when he sitting out on the verandah Sugath arrived.

"Here Mahen, here's the letter," you have to come for an interview tomorrow morning at eight o'clock.

'We have received your application and shall be pleased to see you at an interview –' The words swam before his eyes. The shadows of evening grew darker, pressing down on

19

him. He held the letter in his clammy fingers and wondered, will they really be 'pleased' to see me?

Sugath sat by him. "Mahen", he said, "don't worry *machang*. I'll be there no —so don't worry."

He set the alarm clock by his bed. Will it work? Will I oversleep? He'd told his mother also to wake him up in time. What if she overslept? The night dragged on. He swept off the sheet covering him and went up to his window. Somewhere a dog howled. Or was it a person? That's how they howled when they were left half dead — those people he had shot; till he went back and finished them off, silencing their cries for ever. A sharp draft made him shiver. He went back to bed, lay back and shut his eyes tight. I must sleep, I must sleep, I must get up in time to go for my interview.

"Am I late?" His mother was shaking him awake and the alarm was playing.

"No it's quite early." She turned the alarm off. "Here's some tea for you." As he sipped his tea he thought about the coming day. He had arranged his clothes the night before. The grey slacks and new white shirt and the blue tie. He had spent almost half an hour cleaning and polishing his shoes. Just normal, civilian shoes - not boots. The boots which had gone through so much of walking, through terrain of every kind, through mud, through dust, through bloody and charred human flesh. But today might change all that. I might become a proper civilian again, he thought. I must think positive, as Sugath had urged me to.

He showered and dressed slowly, taking care to do everything perfectly. He combed his hair a dozen times over, and adjusted his collar, and his sweaty fingers slipped and fumbled with his tie knot over and over again. It's so

20

difficult to get this right – he gave it a final tug. He looked at his reflection in the mirror and saw a tall young man, well built, neatly combed hair, white shirt, grey slacks, crooked tie - which he adjusted – quite smart really. Then he saw the face, not his face but some monster's, staring back at him. His mouth felt sour and a cramp wrenched at his insides.

"No no I can't do it," he cried out, "I can't, I can't."
Pulling out his tie and his shirt he flung them on the floor.
He fell on his bed and buried his face in his pillow.
A hand reached out and caressed his head, then a voice spoke. Gently. Like the birdsong.
Putha, it's alright, it's alright.

Moments in Time

She wanted to escape. If she had the freedom to do whatever she wanted, surely she could just step out of the house and disappear? Not disappear in the real sense of the word. Just for a few hours – not forever. It was hard to imagine life without him and the children and the dogs and cats and the servants and all the plants and the trees in the large garden. No, she couldn't really be without them at all. But all she wanted was a few moments to herself, maybe an hour or two, just to feel and observe, undisturbed. People, things, surroundings, all these were drawn to the periphery of her life when she was with others. Then the others became the centre. She was constantly having to listen, talk, reply, suggest, agree, disagree –a gamut of obligations to fulfill. By herself she could just meander, observe, ignore or notice the most insignificant, ponder on the least important with no one to tell her how and why and when. The cords were untied and all that lay between her and everything else was this boundless freedom.

She stepped out of the house, through the back door. The elderly woman who'd been with them for twenty-two years was cooking in the adjoining kitchen, too busy to hear her leave. Her husband was in the office room upstairs, finishing off some report or another. The children were playing around the pool on the far side of the house. She hoped the young girl she'd got from the village to be in charge of them had a sense of responsibility. She hesitated. Would there be any mishaps when she was away? Should she go then? Or stay? She paused. This was ridiculous. Surely one hour of her absence would not create such a calamity? Surely no one would fall into the pool, or burn themselves on the cooker or get a stroke?

Once outside she took a deep breath. It was a release being alone. If someone else were with her there'd be talking, laughing or trying to be polite with each other. She'd have to be absorbed in others, not herself. Now alone she could do her deep breathing. It was something to be done alone. By herself.

The walk through the back gate, gently shutting it into place and proceeding on the small road, was the first part of her journey outside. The branches of some trees bowed low, weighted with the wetness of the night's heavy shower. Birds flew in and out screeching and calling to one another and hordes of yellow butterflies fluttered busily, as if time was running out. Time indeed is running out, she thought wistfully. For all of us, not just for me. But at the moment she was only concerned with herself. Time is running out for me, she thought. She cast her eyes tenderly at the leaves on the trees, the mud that had caked in uneven lumps on the side of the road and the radiant colours of the tiny honey suckers chirping and fluttering around in maddening haste to sip the nectar from the flowers. The flowers themselves, little pink petals which would fall and die and eventually disappear into the earth. Like she would at some point in time. Things would never be exactly the same again and this moment was to be treasured, she thought. But then, each moment is like that, never to happen again.

The path led to the main road. It had been turned into a highway, broad and smooth, its six lanes of traffic caused a rumble similar to thunder. She stopped, watching the enormous container lorries move with startling speed, cars

23

and other vehicles rushing with a purpose. People walked on the pavements, which had also been widened and paved evenly unlike earlier times. Girls dressed in long slim skirts and short blouses, bags slung over their shoulders walked hurriedly - on their way back from work. Schoolchildren in white uniforms carrying bulky back packs moved at lesser pace but still with serious intent written all over their faces. Was school over so late these days? It must be the wretched tuition classes they had to attend. In sharp contrast an old man grasping a stick dragged himself along the pavement. He carried a faded cloth bag in one hand and made his way into a *kade* on the wayside. She watched as he limped inside the shop gave them a few coins and took a loaf of bread in return. He pulled out a *siri siri* bag from the cloth *malla* and put the bread into this, stepped outside, paused for a few moments and once again began his laborious journey.

She passed the new hospital on the opposite side, multi storeyed with its gleaming glass and chrome façade, a building that one could see from miles away. The little houses on her side of the road stood up against each other like biscuit packets. A Sinhala tune drifted from one of them and a child carrying a broken box darted outside followed by a screeching mother. They almost ran into her and had she not stepped aside would certainly have tripped and fallen. A skinny white dog with one black ear and a thin curled up tail lying on the side looked up in alarm at the uproar, then put his head down closed his eyes and went to sleep again. Garbage spilt out from an open bag and grains of rice and pieces of stale curry lay strewn on the side of the road. The stink of rotting fruit made her hold her breath as she walked past quickly. The breathing was so important she realized half smiling to herself. There are some moments to exhale and some to inhale and some just to hold your breath. Now the slums ended and large office buildings emerged on the sides. Large car parks sprawl over the compounds. A line of people of varying ages and sizes gathered at the bus-stop, some stood patiently while others shifted from foot to foot glancing at their watches, waiting for that bus that was always late. She wondered whether she too should climb into a bus and go somewhere, anywhere – wherever it would take her, the last stop. Where would she be then? But no, that's not what she wanted, she would have to concentrate and listen and talk and ask questions, no that wasn't what she wanted at this moment.

She took another deep breath. The air was parched despite the rains last night and the odour of earth and dust drifted up her nostrils. The skies looked sultry again. When she had left they were blue and had white fluffy clouds but in this short while they'd changed. If it rained she would allow herself to get soaked. She'd stand in the rain right in the middle of the pavement and let it pour down her body. Then she would go back home. They'd have a fit at home, they would. The elderly woman in the kitchen would come running out and cry out in horror, and the children would shout about it when they saw her. He'd be too absorbed in his work and not notice her and she could slip into the bathroom and shower and change and go out and greet him as if nothing had happened. A few drops fell, heavily, deliberately. A warning sign. She had to decide. Sighing, she turned back. Her watch indicated the time when the family would be gathering on the verandah for evening tea and she'd better be there. She'd spent almost an hour outside. Time to return to her real world.

A sudden feeling of lightheadedness overcame her. She wanted to do something different. She spotted the ice-cream parlour across the road. It was difficult to cross over but looking to either side carefully, she did. The ice-cream was scrumptious. It had vanilla and mint and chocolate chips in it. Eating it while walking along, made her feel like a schoolgirl, licking the ice-cream as it melted down the cone. Soon it was all over.

The little black wrought iron gate was visible now. Opening it gently she walked to the back and entered the house the same way she'd left. The tea things were laid out on the verandah and the children were just coming in from their swim. The new girl from the village carried the towels ready to put them out to dry in the back garden. She walked up the stairs and went into his study. He was seated at his desk head bent over his work. At the sound of her footsteps he looked up and smiled. It was good to be back.

Better Half

Geetha and Sarath were coming to lunch on Sunday – two days away.

Sharmini's head throbbed. *God I wish they weren't coming – maybe something will stop them.*

"What are we giving them for lunch?" This was the third time Gihan had asked her. "Must give them something good no."

Sharmini scoffed. "Don't I always give them something 'good.' – *but this is typical of Gihan. Such a damn fuss over his sister, she has to have the best always.*

"Remember not to put too much chilli in the chicken curry – *akka* can't take too much of chilli now. Shall we get some prawns also?"

"Chicken and prawns? Isn't that a bit too much? I mean they are both so expensive – wouldn't just chicken be enough?"

Gihan ignored her. "You know *akka* likes that mango chutney – I'll get some."

I'll stuff her big mouth with chutney so she won't be able to talk –ha! Sharmini laughed.

"What's so funny? Every time my family visits you think it's funny. When your sister comes you go all out making this and that."

Sharmini sighed. *My sister, oh my sister- is so different. She's kind and sensitive and – and I love her. But this is your sister! How could I forget all those comments she made when you married me - that I was uneducated and from a poor family?*

"Oh Gihan – don't worry – we'll get something wonderful for lunch. Why are they suddenly coming down from Kandy anyway, anything special?'

27

"We have to meet the lawyer, he's drawing up the division of mother's property."

"Isn't it half shares?"

"Hmm yes, but we have to sort out which half goes to whom."

Sharmini pursed her lips. Oh that woman – she'll definitely take the part she wants. The way she took all her mother's jewellery and the crockery and furniture and left nothing for Gihan. Gihan is far too soft on her. *Loku akka* – big sister – as though she is God or something.

"*Loku Akka* will have to have first choice no Sharmini, after all she is my older sister."

There! I knew he'll say it. How I hate those words. Older sister, older sister – all the time it's a case of her getting everything she wants!

Sharmini was silent while she washed the dishes. I have to be tactful now – very very – diplomatic - is the word. Mustn't upset Gihan – it's impossible to change the way he feels about his sister. He'll agree with whatever she says. I wish we could have a nice little house with a neat front lawn and a bit of garden. This tiny flat is killing me. We're so cooped up here.

It was when Sharmini was cleaning up their flat that she discovered Gihan' drawings of the tree. It looked like the same tree – same kind of trunk with widespread branches and clusters of flowers. Although they were pencil sketches, the tree was unmistakable. It was an araliya tree. Sharmini smiled to herself as she put them together. I wonder what possessed him to draw so many of the same tree?   Must be for the office. Gihan was an artist at an ad agency.

She put all the papers on his desk into the drawer. After all, she couldn't have the place looking untidy when his sister and brother-in-law came to lunch!

The next two days were a flurry of marketing and cooking. Sharmini tidied the house and polished the floor. She woke up early on Sunday and started on the cooking. The day was bright making her tiny kitchen hot and stuffy. It was past eleven when she had finished her work. She hurried into the bathroom to shower and dress up for her visitors.

As soon as she'd dressed Sharmini checked to see that everything was in place. The brilliant coloured croton she had bought at the Viharamahadevi Park sale last week glowed in the corner of the compact sitting room. Even the small round dining table looked quite elegant with the white plates and blue napkins. Everything was ready!

"It's almost twelve fifteen – they said they would come at twelve." Gihan grumbled, peering at his watch. Some minutes later the doorbell rang, making him leap off his chair and rush to the door.
Geetha and Sarath stood there – in their designer jeans and tee shirts, and their dark glasses which covered their eyes so well you couldn't say where they were looking. But Sharmini knew they were taking in the flat, noticing the cheap chintz curtains, and the dull furniture. She reluctantly returned their on-the-cheek sniffs, knowing well that they were doing this through a sense of duty rather than love. The whiff of expensive perfume drifted through the flat.

They filled the small sitting room - with its single sofa and two armchairs. After a round of drinks the subject of the Will came up.

"So we better have lunch now *malli*, if we are to meet the lawyer at two.'

Gihan looked across at Sharmini.

"Ah yes – I'll have it ready in no time at all." She smiled and rose from her chair.

The minute kitchen was just a few steps away and while warming the food Sharmini was able to catch snippets of conversation from the sitting room.

First Geetha's voice. "So *malli* – we have to decide what to tell the lawyer no – about the division. I don't know why *amma* didn't divide it properly - now we have to take the decision."

Gihan –"Well at least we have something – what's so difficult about taking a decision on what each of us should get?"

Sarath- "Anyway as Geetha is the older of you both, I think she should have the first choice no?"

Sharmini stopped what she was doing and muttered under her breath. There we are again. I knew they'd come up with that older sister business. She arranged the dishes on the table and poured water into the glasses. The other three were still seated – she noticed that Gihan was breaking his knuckles, a sure sign of irritation.

"Come – lunch is ready." They were too wrapped up in their thoughts and didn't even hear her. Sharmini repeated "Come and eat now – before the food gets cold."

They sauntered to the table and sat down with hardly a glance at the food.

"Here akka – some mango chutney that you like so much. And I remembered not to put too much chillie in the chicken curry also." Sharmini beamed. She served some onto Geetha's plate.

Gihan stared at her. What's this? Sharmini's actually being polite to my sister!

"So have you'll decided how you're going to divide the property?"

Gihan could hardly believe what he heard. She never interfered with my family matters? What's got into her?

Geetha spoke, "No not yet. I can't decide."

Later when they were having their dessert, Sharmini passed the bowl of fruit and ice cream to her sister in law. The two men had left the table to watch the cricket match on their small television set.

"So which part does *malli* like Sharmini?"

Sharmini steadied herself as a million thoughts raced through her head. "Well he's always talking about the house. I'll also be so happy to have a nice house and all that lovely old furniture."

Geetha stared at her. After a long pause she said, "I thought Gihan liked the garden. when he was a kid he was mad about that araliya tree. I remember he used to be climbing it all the time – I tried it once and nearly fell down. It used to be full of those *dimiyas* also uggh."

Something snapped in Sharmini's head. The tree – of course – the araliya tree! She thought hard. "But the garden is like a jungle now. Such a mess." she screwed up her nose. "It must be so noisy also as it's closer to the main road." She cleared the dishes as she spoke. Geetha followed her into the kitchen.

"So then you think he prefers the house? You also like the house?"

"Oh yes." Sharmini looked at her and smiled. "Geetha why don't you go and watch the match? I'll bring your coffee there."

"No no I don't want coffee. Anyway- I'll strain my eyes on such a small TV set. We're used to a big one no, the picture is so clear on ours."

"Of course, that must be lovely."

Geetha glanced at her watch. *"Malli,* we'd better get moving, it's 1.40 already. Let's go, otherwise we'll be late."
Sharmini dried her hands and came up to them as they were leaving.
Gihan avoided her eyes, he didn't want her to say something strange again.

Sharmini put away the dishes and sat down with the newspapers. Somehow she found it difficult to concentrate. She thought of the old house. She remembered its musty rooms and dark corridors, and how its wooden beams had begun to rot and cracks had appeared in some of the alls. They must be sitting there in front of the lawyer, arguing like mad – or maybe as usual Gihan will take the *malli* role and just keep mum. Of course *Loku Akka* will be bossing everyone – even the lawyer, and Sarath will see to it that they get the maximum out of it all.

Nearly two hours had passed and still Gihan hadn't returned. Shall I call him on his mobile? Or no – he might get annoyed, especially if he's in the middle of the discussion.
 She swept and tidied the place, propping up the cushions and adjusting the covers on the chairs. She picked up the papers again and sat down with them. The words and pictures just flitted past her eyes. Oh damn! Where is he? She looked at her watch. She was about to get up and go into the kitchen to make herself a cup of tea when she heard footsteps outside. Before he could ring the bell she was at the door. She flung it open and there he stood, looking exhausted.
"Gihan," she cried, "what happened?"
"Well she got what she wanted – so I guess she was happy about it."
He slumped on the sofa and stretched out his legs.

"So what did she get?" she spoke slowly, trying to hide her impatience.

"Well as she said to me '*Malli* – que sera sera – what will be will be – you must accept what you get' – how do you like that bit of speechifying from her?"

"So then - what happened?"

"And can you believe it - she was saying that you liked the house. Such rubbish! I argued so much my throat is dry, just trying to tell her that you had nothing to do with this and in any case you didn't like the damn house and that I didn't either. Then she said that I was a liar – can you imagine – that I was a 'scheming liar like my wife' – I could've clobbered her I tell you. She's really lost her mind, that sister of mine!" He opened the fridge and yanked out a bottle of iced water.

Sharmini passed him a glass.

"Also, the house has more land with it than the plot in front – three perches more. Can you imagine? She went on and on about the three perches. Saying that you and I wanted the house because of the extra land. Such nonsense! I felt like just walking out."

"So then – then what?"

"Oh God – I don't want to talk about it. The house the house, the whole damn conversation was about the house. I must have a shower and cool off. I feel totally drained after all that!"

"But Gihan – what –"

Gihan sat down and closed his eyes.

"Doesn't matter Gihan – " Sharmini said as she sat by him, "we'll work it out. I know it'll be a huge job to do up the house – but –"

"The house?"

"Why? Didn't Akka give you the house?"

"The house? My God – how could you be so dumb?"

"You mean she didn't ..?"

"Nonsense! She was so sure that we wanted the house that she took it."

"So then you got - the garden? "her voice was a whisper. There was a tight feeling in her chest.

"Ya - I was so damn taken aback - I could've dropped!"

Sharmini remained silent, too dumbfounded to speak. Images sped through her mind. "Ah – so that v̵ ̵s the tree – now I know."

"Tree? What tree?" he laughed.

New Shoes

Today I am going to Prema Auntie's. I was placed sixth in the whole Island in the Grade Five Scholarship Exam. Now I have a chance to go to a big school in Colombo. I was the talk of the village. People came up to me and patted me under my chin, "Clever boy, clever boy" they would say to me, squeezing my cheeks till they hurt. When my father told Prema Auntie the good news she was very happy and asked me to stay with her, so I could attend my new school which was close to her house. Prema Auntie was not a real aunt - but her family and ours were connected, my father told me, so I called her 'Auntie'. It was too complicated for me to understand, the connection I mean. But Prema Auntie used to visit us in the village sometimes when she visited other relations in that area. She would bring us lots of gifts and some nice toys and clothes for me and my family.

My mother always said, "Prema of course is not stuck up like all your other relations — they only like to be in the city, they are ashamed of their 'gamay' relatives." She would make chooking and chukking sounds with her mouth as she said this, and my father would mumble "Why are you so worried about these things? Now see, our son has got into a fine school, just be happy about that." Then she'd stop whatever she was doing, and look at me and smile.

My mother packed everything into two large polythene bags which made a chiri-chiri sound each time she touched them. I got three new white shirts and navy blue shorts. My uncle gave me a new sarong for passing the exam, so that was also put in. My father took me to the big shoe shop in town and bought me a pair of shoes. I had never worn shoes before, not real closed ones although I did have a pair of sandals, but these looked nice and shiny and I was eager to put them on. But when I did, they were so uncomfortable! My feet were totally crushed by them. My father said that in Colombo all the boys wore shoes, therefore I had to do the same.

My two younger sisters stood staring at me with sad looks on their faces. Their cheeks were wet as I said goodbye to them. My aunt and uncle and my cousins who lived nearby had gathered to see me off. Then I went to my grandmother. She must have been about a hundred years old, bent low and with white hair tied into a knot at the back of her neck. I fell on my knees before her, asking her blessings.

The bus journey wasn't comfortable. We stopped so many times - the trip took hours. I had to stand all the way. But I managed to lean against my mother and take the weight of my feet which were now sore and aching. The new shoes were cutting into the back of my feet and I wished so much I could just take them off. But my father insisted I kept them on, to look presentable for Prema Auntie, he said. Not just a village boy. But I was a village boy, I insisted, trying to wriggle my toes in these horrid contraptions. My parents just looked at me. I was going to Colombo, they intoned. The Big City. I was no longer a village boy.

At last the bus groaned to a halt. We had reached our destination. I carried the bag with my things and mother carried the other one. She had filled it with kavum, kokis and kalu dodol, and the biggest bunch of koli-kuttus from the garden. My father carried his black umbrella even though it didn't look like it was going to rain.

Colombo was a city with many huge buildings. Some of them were so tall I could hardly see the top of them! Cars, buses, bicycles, and all kinds of vehicles and plenty of those tuk-tuks with three wheels crowded the roads. People were all over, like ants crawling on the ledge underneath my window at home, all rushing this way and that. We had to take another bus to get to Prema Auntie's. Soon we were there. We stepped out onto a wide pavement. I was happy to see some big flamboyant trees with fire coloured flowers and even a giant bo tree in the centre of the road. We turned down a quiet shady road where Prema Auntie lived. Her house had an enormous black gate and very high walls. I had never seen such high walls before. And for a house, what for? My father pointed to a button on the wall and explained that it was the bell for the house. An electric bell! I reached out and pressed hard. My father pulled my hand down when I tried to press it again.

"You only press it once." he said.

"But how do you know it rang inside? " I hadn't heard any sound at all. The bell in the temple was so large and made such a clanging sound, we could hear it for miles around! And here, this tiny button was supposed to ring a bell inside the house?

" Of course it would have rung inside." my father replied.

Minutes ticked by with no response.

I plucked up my courage, "Shall I press it again?"

"Hmm." replied my father nodding his head.

I reached up again and put my finger really hard on the little button which had so much power behind it.

Soon we heard a rattle at the gate. A little peephole slid open and a pair of eyes peered out at us.

"Aah" said a gruff voice, and with a click the gate was opened for us.

"So, you have brought the boy." Piyadasa the old gardener greeted my father.

We were asked to go to the back verandah and wait for my aunt. My father removed his slippers and my mother did the same, and to my immense joy I was told to remove my shoes before we entered the house. I stretched my feet and wriggled my toes up and down. It felt so delightful not to have them all stuck together. The black nylon socks had made my feet all damp and sweaty. I left the shoes on the steps of the house, happy to be rid of them!

We walked across the front verandah which had lots of chairs on either side facing one another, and big pots of plants all along the edge. Then we entered a large hall where carpets covered the floor and felt soft and fluffy under my bare feet. There were plenty of large black carved chairs and tables. Huge brass bowls filled with flowers stood on the tables. Great big paintings and lots of photographs decorated the walls. An enormous lamp hung from the high ceiling. – it looked more like those big lanterns I make during Vesak, only thing was it was made out of glass. I couldn't stop gazing at the lovely colours of the tiny pieces of glass as they caught a thin ray of sunlight that streamed into the room. The next room had a long table with chairs around it. Dark wooden cupboards and tables stood against the walls, over which more pictures and photographs hung.

The back verandah which opened out into the garden was filled with sunlight. Prema Auntie came to us saying "Hullo hullo come come." in a loud and jolly way. She was dressed in a long dress in a batik design. My father and mother greeted her bowing slightly with their hands clasped together. I knelt down at her feet and she touched my head. She smiled at me and called me to her side. I inhaled a sweet smell when she hugged me.

"So this clever son of yours is going to the biggest school in Colombo! I have made an appointment with the Principal and we can go there in a little while. But you must be tired, so have a cool drink first."

A boy brought us drinks on a silver tray. The drink was very cold and sweet. I gulped it down almost choking on its iciness.

Now we had to meet the Principal. I felt excited and anxious at the same time. The worst part was that I had to put on the horrid shoes and socks again. We all climbed into Prema Auntie's car. It was quite cold inside. The back seat was so large that when I leaned back my feet hung in mid-air. Prema Auntie and my mother sat with me at the back. My father sat in front with the driver Gunapala. My mother sat at the edge and clutched onto the top of the front seat. Father just leaned back, looking like he had owned a car all his life. I shut my eyes for a moment. It was like floating on air.

The school was huge! I had never seen anything like it. It was even bigger than Prema Auntie's house and much bigger than the hospital in the town near our village. I could easily get lost in this place. We sat outside the Principal's office. There were so many boys in this school - thousands! I couldn't believe it, why my village school had ninety two children and consisted of one large hall which was divided into classrooms. Most often we sat under a tree and did our lessons.

The door opened and we faced the Principal. He was dressed in a long sleeved shirt and tie and long trousers. I thought of my former Principal who wore a white sarong and long shirt. While he was talking to my parents and to Prema Auntie, whom he seemed to know quite well, I glanced down and noticed he wore black shoes like mine. He seemed to be quite comfortable in them. Maybe in time I would get used to my shoes too. He told me he was sure I would bring great honour to the school. My parents and Prema Auntie beamed at me. I could see hordes of boys outside. They were talking and laughing and running around. We were shown the classrooms. Desks and chairs in rows, all stiff and straight. They looked very unfriendly and I ached for my village school and my old friends Senaka and Sunil; for the big tamarind tree in the compound where I used to collect the fallen fruit and stuff them into my pockets to eat on the way back home; for the river that flowed behind the school where we used to swim and play. But no more of that now. All of a sudden I felt cold and my stomach began to hurt.

"I hope you are going to be happy here." the Principal said to me.

"I'm sure he will." said Prema Auntie.

"Yes of course." my father echoed.

My mother said nothing. She just looked at me.

On the way back she put her arm around me, something she rarely did.

Prema Auntie took us to a large room off the back verandah.

"This is your bedroom," she smiled and patted me on the head.

It had a bed with a mattress and pillows and sheets and all that. A large cupboard with two doors stood in the corner for my clothes and things. My few belongings barely filled half a shelf. I wondered what I was going to put in the rest of the cupboard. There was a table with a mirror attached to it and my comb looked so bleak and lonely on its large surface. At one end was yet another table with drawers running down on both sides in front.

"This is your desk." said Prema Auntie rather proudly. "It's a very old one and I used it when I went to school." Enough of room for my books and pencils and pens - and so many other things I would have to take to school now!

The bathroom was at the end of the verandah. I had never seen a bathroom like that; it had a raised up toilet with a wooden seat and cover, a white washbasin, and a special place for the shower enclosed with a green plastic curtain. Bathing under the shower would be like standing in the rain. We used to have rainbaths in the village, such fun falling in the mud and having the rain pelting down our bodies! Prema Auntie had a thick cloth on the floor, and a nice blue towel on the rail.

We sat down to a late lunch. There were little squares of cloth beside each plate. Piyadasa served the food to each person separately. There was rice with cadjunuts and raisins in it, chicken curry and many other curries. Tasty, but not as nice as *amma's* cooking. The tumbler by my plate had iced water which I liked very much. I gulped it down and *amma* nudged me and shook her head. Before I could even put my glass down Piyadasa came over to refill it. This time I didn't gulp it down but took small sips like Prema Auntie did. After that we had chocolate ice-cream which just melted in my mouth. Prema Auntie told Piyadasa to serve me more ice-cream but again my mother nudged me so I said I was full and couldn't eat any more, thank you.

Prema Auntie told me that if I worked hard maybe I could become a doctor or a lawyer some day and have a big car and a big house. With all these thoughts flashing through my head I felt a bit better.

"Come let me show you the garden," she said. The lawn was like a carpet - so smooth and neat and green that I felt

41

reluctant to step on it. At the far corner I was delighted to find a pond where there were many different types of fish.

"See - that's a carp," said Prema Auntie, pointing to a pale golden fish, "and those are guppies - they eat the mosquito eggs so they are useful in the pond."

Piyadasa was sweeping the garden and came down to the pond to feed the fish.

As he neared the pond the fish swam hurriedly to meet him at the edge - it was almost like they had recognised him!

Soon I found myself chatting to him about the fish. We suddenly realised that it was dinner time and walked back to the house.

"Tomorrow you can feed the fish," she promised with a smile. "After dinner I have a surprise for you."

I couldn't wait for dinner to be over.

She held out a large green school bag. It was one of those things you carried on your back. I touched it and it felt smooth, almost silky. The buckles on the straps shone. I couldn't wait to fill it with my books and take it to school. Even the thought of wearing my new shoes didn't seem so bad after all.

After that we went to our bedroom for the night. My mother shared the bed with me, and my father slept on a folding bed Piyadasa set up in the room. Soon they were fast asleep but I lay awake thinking of all the things at home. I missed my mat and my old soft pillow. I missed my dog Laki who used to sleep near my feet. I must've fallen asleep past midnight. I woke up to my mother shaking me. "Get up *putha*, you have to get ready for school."

School! I wished I didn't have to go. Everything happened so quickly, the shower, wearing my new clothes, having breakfast at the big dining table. We were going in Prema Auntie's car to school. She came out to the verandah to see us off. "You're looking very smart. I'll come today with Gunapala to pick you up after school, alright?"

Dressed in my new white shirt, dark blue shorts and new shoes that still pinched slightly I walked through the gates with my green knapsack strung across my back. My parents took me to the office where an older boy wearing a tie with a silver badge on it took me to my classroom. There were groups of boys gathered at the entrance chattering and laughing with one another. My parents looked at me with a mixture of pride and sadness in their faces. My eyes began to sting as with a quick wave I went inside.

The Peon

The first thing Kumara saw when he awoke was his uniform, hanging on two large nails by the door. A beige shirt with the company's initials embroidered on the pocket, and dark brown trousers.

He could hear Seeelawathie moving around. She would be boiling a kettle of water for their morning tea. He turned over and saw her walk over to where their two children, ten year old Saman and six year old Manel, were curled up on their mats, fast asleep just across from him.

"Get up, get up - you will all be late -" she shook the children and looked at Kumara."Get up," she repeated.

Today was the day he had planned to go to the shops to buy them some clothes for the Festival which was in two weeks' time. He got up quickly, as he didn't want to get late for work, not today of all days, and gulped down the steaming cup of tea Seelawathie put in front of him. The children and he bathed at the road tap close by and had their breakfast of *roti* and *sambol* before they dressed.

"*Thaththi* are you bringing us new clothes for the festival?" the children asked their eyes gleaming.

"Yes - of course."

Seelawathie just looked at him - she knew they had spent most of his salary this month.

"*Thaththi* let's see the keys again." Saman said. They were not large jangling keys, but small ones which made no sound at all, not even when Saman knocked them against each other. Manel took them and felt them with her little fingers.

"Ah ha - now don't lose them - otherwise -finished -"said Kumara.

"Why *thaththi?*" they asked him for the millionth time. Every morning they would ask him this question and he would give them the same reply.

"Look," he said to them, "I have to go early to open the office - if I don't go no one can get in. Why they would have to close the office for the whole day   wouldn't that be a joke!"

"*Thaththi* is the boss - if he doesn't go no one can get in!" the children laughed.

Kumara peered into the small mirror on the wall and ran a dirty toothless comb through his hair and then put his worn out purse and keys into a special pocket Seelawathie had sewn into the inside waist of his trousers.

There was hardly anyone at the bus stop at six fifteen that morning. After about ten minutes he got into an almost empty bus. As it wound through the maze of roads in the half light of the new day, the city was beginning to come to life. School children sauntered in small groups, white uniformed, carrying books and water bottles, and office workers were also beginning to enter the bus as they proceeded. The shops in Maradana from where he planned to buy the clothes for Seelawathie and the children, were all closed. It took more than an hour to reach Kumara's office in the heart of the city. When he saw the tall buildings with the sunlight bouncing off the glass and chrome windows, he knew he was near his office. Soon they passed the modern skyscrapers and moved into an older part of the city where his office stood.

He stood in front of the office door and slipped in the first key - there were two locks to be opened. It took a firm but gentle turn to open the first lock. Then he pressed the second key into the keyhole above this. This was the tricky one, with the double lock. So turn and turn again - click,

click. The large wooden door moved slightly and the early morning light slowly entered the rooms. Kumara went inside, picked up two old buckets and filled them off the kitchen tap. Then taking the mop from behind the door he went into the main office to begin his work.

The office looked strange with no one there, all those empty seats and no sound at all.
"Oh ho" said Kumara to no one "Here I come cleaning -here I come cleaning - everyone move out of the way." He rolled along as if he were on roller skates. He marched up to his boss's room and opened the door with a swing."Ho ho-" he shouted as he took the curve behind the large wooden desk. Pulling out the chair with one hand he pressed the mop up and down under the desk with the other. "All done sir- how's that sir?" Then, he threw down the mop, sat in the chair and swivelled himself round and round. He spoke in a deep voice that sounded something like his boss's. "Kumara - what is it you want? Ah - come and meet me later. Kumara - I have just promoted you - from tomorrow you are going to be made the accountant - you can sit at Mohan's desk - because I have sacked Mohan the rogue! Ha ha!"

He finished mopping the floor, cleaned everything in the room, and marched to Mohan's cubicle. Mohan was the accountant in the firm. He was the only person other than the boss to have a separate room. "Remember to knock before you come in and close the door after you go out." he barked at everyone. He was always adding and subtracting long lists of numbers, pouring over large sheets of paper, his head bent and his glasses falling over his nose. But now - now Mohan's vacant chair looked sad and lonely. Kumara sat down hard on it. "Hah Mister Mohan- how are you?" Kumara whined in Mohan's whiney voice. He pulled

Mohan's 'In' tray and rummaged through the papers - he picked up some envelopes "The Manager, Bank of Ceylon - The Manager, Lanka Paint Works -Ah Kumara - here take these to them immediately   - hurry up - they are very urgont." Mohan's high pitched squeaky voiced gushed out of Kumara's throat. "Hurry up hurry up." Kumara squeaked as he got up from the chair and ran around the desks, pushing his mop up and down furiously.

He stopped. "Ah Sharmi Missie - how are you?" he spoke to the unoccupied desk of Sharmi the Secretary. He tried the drawers on Sharmi's desk but they were all locked. He put the duster across his left shoulder and twisted and turned as he walked. "My name - Sharmi - hullo everybody." he mimicked in Sharmi's affected voice adding a giggle at the end.

He went back to the mop and pail. Only twenty minutes before the others came in - he had better finish soon. He switched on the air conditioners so that the place would be cool when the people came in.

"Now I am finished - everybody say 'tankyou Mister Kumara'. The empty office remained mute. "Tank you MISTER Kumara SIR- tank you tank you Sir." He held the mop facing him and bowed low as he spoke.

The door creaked with the constant opening and closing as the employees began to come in. Kumara was seated in his usual place- on the green aluminium chair in the tiny kitchen at the back. Every day at ten o'clock he made tea for the office staff. After he poured the tea he added the milk and sugar into it, stirred it vigourously, and then poured it into the cups, holding the jug about a foot high so that the pale brown liquid gushed down, frothing up in the cups. Someone was calling him, but he pretended not to hear - he didn't want anyone or anything to disturb his tea making. He'd put the twelve cups of tea on a big tray to take them around the office, placing a cup carefully on each desk. There were always a few tea leaves and spoons of sugar which he managed to save to take home – hiding them in his inner pocket.

"Kumara are you deaf - I called you so many times - where were you?" Miss Sharmi was in a bad mood already. Her voice had reached the squeaky stage. By the end of the day she probably would have lost it completely. Hope she does, he thought. Silly woman, look at her waving her sari pota up and down and screaming at me.

"I'll report you to the Boss if you go on like this." the squeak took such a high that the last few words disappeared down her throat.

Kumara couldn't afford to be reported -whatever else happened - not with the Festival coming along. He couldn't get into trouble now.

"Aiyo Missi so sorry - I was in the tea room - making the tea, making Missi's tea also-" he put down the tea gingerly on her table. She pouted and sat down not speaking a word.

He went into Mohan's room. "Knock on the door Kumara - how many times to tell you? I have some letters to be delivered immediately, all right - go straight away, all right - these are all urgent." Mohan was rattling on and on. His whole life was on one long Urgent mode.

"Sir - I'll serve the tea and then go sir."

"Hurry up hurry up - you're so slow maybe we should get a new peon to do this for us -"

Kumara put the cup down hurriedly and spilt some tea into the saucer.

Mohan shrieked again - "See now you have spilt my tea - next time you'll spill it on some important document."

Kumara hurriedly passed on the other cups and came back to Mohan's desk.

"What! You haven't still gone? Quickly take these and go-"
he thrust the envelopes out like daggers. Kumara put them
into his satchel, got onto his bicycle and pedalled away.
He breathed in deeply when he got out of the office. It was
good to be outside even though it was crowded and noisy.
There was no one to shout at him- do this, do that- all the
time. He checked the addresses on the letters and worked
out his route.

Halfway, the heat got to him and he stopped for a cool
drink at a *saiwa kade*. The *vades* looked tempting but he
didn't have the money to buy any, so he just sighed and
went back to delivering his letters.

The cold air hit him as he entered the office. He went into
his little place in the kitchen and sat down.

"Kumara, Mr Mohan wants you-"

He ran his fingers through his hair and adjusted his
uniform before he went into Mohan's cubicle.

He knocked on the door and opened it slightly, but Mohan
was talking on the phone. He looked at Kumara and
ignored him. Kumara stood outside and peeped in from
time to time.

"Kumara - what do you want? Can't you see I'm busy?"

"Sir - you sent for me sir."

"Ah yes. Now what was it? Ah yes - these salary advances
you are taking - they have to stop - you are now taking
advances on the next month's salary - this won't do."

Kumara looked down and said nothing.

"Do you understand?"

Kumara nodded although he didn't understand. After all,
it was his money, so what did it matter when he took it?
But Mohan was the Accountant and without his approval
he couldn't get any money from the office. The boss was the
boss and didn't look into all these small things. What about
the festival advance? Should he ask for it?

"Sir - what about -"

"What about what?" Mohan shouted. The phone rang and he picked it up. Kumara waited.

"What?" Mohan snapped, finishing his call.

"Festival advance sir - for the New Year."

"New Year? That's a long way off - about two weeks more. Anyway, you have taken almost your whole salary for this month - I can't be giving you money like this - you have to be taught a lesson - no advance this time for the New Year. If you go on like this, we'll have to tell you to leave. This nonsense can't go on."

Kumara stumbled out - everything seemed a blur. He sat on his green aluminum chair and scratched his head. What if they sacked him? Would he be able to get another job? What would happen to the children - they might have to stop school, and Seelawathie might have to work - but then who would be at home?

"Kumara - Kumara - you are really deaf - I have been calling you so many times." Miss Sharmi looked all red and puffed up like she did when she lost her temper.

" The boss wants you to wash his car before you go this evening. Now do it properly for heaven's sake."

Kumara had to make more tea in the afternoon and deliver more letters too.

He returned about fifteen minutes before the office closed for the day and was washing the car when the boss came down.

"Ah Kumara- still doing the car? You won't have time to go shopping for New Year!" the boss laughed.

"Not going shopping sir."

"Why?"

Kumara pursed his lips. Should he say about the Festival Advance being cancelled by Mohan? He took a deep breath.

"No money sir - Mr Mohan don't give any Festival Advance

sir, " the boss looked surprised, so Kumara went on, "my fault sir, I take too much advances, my fault sir."

"Oh-"was all the boss said.

Kumara concentrated on wiping the car dry his head a whirl of thoughts. He might get sacked for telling on Mr Mohan and then what?

He was putting the bucket away and squeezing out the rag when there was a tap on his shoulder.

"Ah here Kumara- you take this for New Year - get your family something." Kumara stared hard at the five hundred rupee note thrust in his face.

"But Mr Mohan said sir -"

"Oh that- that's office stuff -"the boss said under his breath." Here -this is from me- okay?"

Kumara could hardly lift his hands to take the money. His fingers turned stiff and quite unbendable. The sound of the car taking off seemed very far away. He stood there for maybe five minutes or five hours - he couldn't tell. Then, very slowly, he folded the note and put it into his purse. His feet hardly touched the ground as he walked to the front door. In went the key- the two click clicks and the other click sounded like the fireworks they lit for the Festival! He didn't mind that he had to wait half an hour for a bus, nor the fact that he had to hang on to the footboard when he finally got one. He leapt off the bus at Maradana. As he walked along he was dazzled by the rows of coloured skirts and blouses, trousers and little dresses hanging up in the shops by the road. They waved in the breeze, as if they were calling him. He squared his shoulders and laughed as he moved towards them.

The Swing

I saw it as soon as I stepped into the garden. A swing, hanging from the mango tree in the far corner. I was drawn to it like a dog to a bone. I hardly heard what the men and women around me were saying. It was one of those business parties I usually dreaded as having to dress up and going to the hairdresser was something I could never be bothered with, but at least this was held in a garden and not in a cloistered chandeliered room of some five star glitz. Nibbling into a minute round of bread topped with some undetectable delicacy, I walked slowly towards the swing, mesmerized as it appeared and disappeared in between the brightly hued saris and shirts and the coloured lights which hung like painted fruit from the mango tree.

As I came nearer I saw that the rough wooden seat was full of holes and the ropes were frayed. I wondered who had used this swing and why it was left to rot like this. I longed to sit on it, to grab the ropes and kick my toes into the grass which would set me off like a pendulum, up and down up and down. Like the old days.

The old days, childhood days, my sister and I - and the swing. We had two swings in our garden so we could go on them together. How we used to run to the swings every afternoon, straight after school, screaming and shouting as my long legs tore ahead. I was always tall for my age and at twelve I towered over my six year old sibling. At first we would sit on the swings and move gently, up and down up and down. Then I would stand on the plank and dare her to do the same.
"I can't, I'll fall." she'd cry.

"Oh don't be such a baby!"

Then she would take a deep breath and stand, gingerly at first, but with each knee bend and the build up of momentum she would become bolder and laugh blithely, watching me all the time to spot any trick I might have hidden from her. I was the export and she the pupil

"Look." I'd say, as I bent my knees, creating a thrust that sent me high into the branches of the mango tree. The leaves would rustle against my face daring me to kiss their tender buds. The wind would brush against my skin and the creak of the rope on the branch would make a grating noise in rhythm with my movements; up and down, up and down. Sunlight would blaze into my eyes. Come, it said, I will jump into your head and give you a halo. I laughed at the thought; what would my family say if I returned to the house with a halo glowing over my head? I laughed out loud and my girl giggles disappeared into the mango tree, rushing out into nowhere, everywhere.

The scream tore sharply through the bubbling sound of my laughter, making the leaves curl and cringe; the sun dimmed and the wind stopped singing. Voices, strident piercing voices, cut through; shouting, shrieking and suddenly the swing stopped. A hand held onto the rope and another held me, pulling me down.

"Silly stupid girl! Look what you've done." My aunt was howling and shaking me by my shoulders at the same time.

"What?" I murmured, my head still dazed with the swinging.

"Look." She caught my chin and turned my face towards the ground. My mother was kneeling over a crumpled white thing lying there on the grass. My sister in her white dress. What was she doing lying down like that? She had been seated on the swing next to me.

"Let's see who can go higher." I'd said.

"I can, I can." She'd cried out her voice cracking with excitement.

While I was up in the leaves and kissing the sunshine, she lost her balance and fell. I hadn't even heard her cry out as her head struck against the boulder. The next few days were filled with tears and whispers. Then she stopped breathing, they told me. Her heart had stopped working and she had gone to Jesus, my mother said. I had never seen my father cry, and was startled to see the way he sobbed aloud, tears streaming down his cheeks, just like we did when we were hurt or sad or upset. I wept against my mother's face and her salty tears mingled with mine. I buried my face in her arms, in her chest, in her lap breathing in the smell of Lavender soap and Snowflake suds. She stood like a wall which separated me from the outside world. My head felt as if it was full of stones and my mouth tasted like cough medicine.

A few days later my father cut down the swings and hurled them into the stream that flowed by our house. I hid behind the mango tree and watched them disappear into the silent murky waters.

I was never allowed to go on a swing again. Never allowed to even mention its name. The mango tree looked bare and empty and so was I. Why did my sister have to die? I hated the swing for taking her in its rope arms and dashing her to death.

Throughout my school life and even as a young adult I never dared touch a swing. When I came across them in parks and playgrounds I ran away pretending I hadn't seen them. When my friends rushed to grab a swing in a garden I'd get one of my migraines and be excused. As I grew up I became adept at spotting a swing a mile away. It became a kind of game for me, if I spotted one I played my part so perfectly, no one knew the truth.

I never thought today would be the day I would actually see one and walk up to it and touch it without being told not to. But at thirty two who was going to tell me not to touch a swing? Sounded ridiculous. Suddenly it was there, in front of me. My body went hot and cold at the sight of it so close. Would I dare? Would I dare walk up to it and touch it and sit on it in front of all those glittering guests? I reached out and touched the ropes, and their rough fibres grazed my well groomed hands. I put my manicured fingers with their dark red nails into the holes on the planks. Hey, look at me I'm a swinger – isn't that funny – I silently cried out. I can swing so high, higher than anyone here. So high, I could catch the moon and the stars. But suddenly tears stung my eyes and I had to dab my eyes quickly before they rolled down my face. I'll never get her back. Never. It was the swing that did it you know, not me. It caught her in its rough ropes and threw her down. I didn't do anything to her, I swear I didn't.

A hand on my shoulder made me turn around sharply. My old schoolfriend Nilmini was gazing at me, a puzzled look in her eyes.
"Are you okay? You look ill."
I swallowed hard and held on to her. The bright lights, multi coloured saris and shirts swirled like a merry-go-round through my moist eyes, human voices buzzed incoherently around me.
"No – it's nothing. I'm fine, just a little dizzy – must be the heat." I steadied my hand and reached out for a glass of iced lemon juice from a passing waiter.

Nilmini led me to a chair and I looked at her and smiled. "I'm okay really."

She sat beside me and kicked off her high heeled shoes. "My feet are aching!"

Thoughts were streaming through my head and my whole body felt clammy. For the first time in years I had actually touched a swing recalling the incidents of that terrible day.

"Do you want to talk?" Nilmini lay her hand on mine.

I hesitated, reluctant to open the festered wounds of the past. The pain came back in a rush and my head began to throb. I clenched my fingers and began. "You know Nilmini, once I had a sister." Suddenly I began to feel lighter, as if a great weight had been taken off me.

The Mango Tree

Sita sat in her wheelchair, awaiting the cup of tea which Mala promised almost an hour ago. Over the last few years chronic arthritis had seeped into her limbs making them twisted and swollen. The pain was unbearable sometimes. But today the strong painkillers seemed to have worked.

She gazed at the mango tree outside - the sapling she had planted fifteen years ago, which had given her many luscious crops. But as she looked, Sita gasped in dismay, for the tree next to it had grown enormous. Its unwieldy branches smothered almost the entire mango tree.

"Mala." she called

"What?" said Mala, bringing the cup of tea. She placed it carelessly on the table spilling some of its contents

"I want to get that big tree felled so that there will be more room for the mango tree."

"I told Kumara to cut down the mango tree, it's useless now - we never get any fruits from it."

"No!" cried Sita, "You must never cut my mango tree."

Mala strode off in a huff.

Sita sipped the tea. and grimaced at its cloying sweetness. How could Mala have forgotten that she couldn't take sugar! But she said nothing, not wanting another altercation with Mala.

She rested her eyes on this matronly woman who stalked the corridors of her house, and recalled how Mala came to her ten years ago. A slightly built, timid girl.

Sita remembered Mala crying.

"It's my sister, her husband died and the inlaws have asked her to leave. She and her little boy have nowhere to go." Mala sobbed.

Sita's heart grieved for them.

"Mala," she said, "they can come here."

The following week Chula and her son Kumara arrived. Chula resembled Mala in her slender build and quiet ways. Kumara was a lively ten years old.
Sita loved having a child in the house! She did up the old store room for them. She found a school nearby for Kumara, and delighted in buying him his books and clothes.
Chula helped Mala with the household chores.
But those days were gone. Polished floors and gleaming furniture had given way to grime and dust. Chula hardly cleaned the house these days. There she was now, cutting some material at the dining table, dragging the scissor along its wooden surface. Kumara whiled away his time sleeping late and listening to loud music.
Sita's eyes stung as she observed the unkempt scene before her.
The doorbell rang. It was her friend Sushila.
"What's it?" she inquired, sensing Sita was upset.
"It's - my mango tree, they want to cut it. It's the other tree that should be chopped." her words came out in a flurry.
"I will arrange that." said Sushila.
It took some hours to fell the tree. First they trimmed the branches and then got to the main trunk. Finally, only the stump was left. The mango tree could now be seen clearly. Its branches were bare and scraggy, and hung with an air of despondency.
Mala watched, her face sombre.

Some weeks later when Sushila visited, she found Sita greatly excited.
"Sushila, look - there are so many new branches and leaves on the mango tree!"

Sita glowed with exhilaration. Indeed, the tree had sprouted several fresh shoots with tender green leaves.

They sat in amicable silence.

Then Sushila spoke - softly, "Sita - intruders stifle - you must get rid of them.".

Sita nodded. "I know - but -I'm scared ."

"It's for your own good," said Sushila, laying her hand on Sita's shoulder. "I'll help you."

Sita hesitated for a few moments. Then she called out firmly. "Mala, I have to speak to you."

Wednesdays & Weekends

Wednesdays are like being in the middle of a suspension bridge. I am in the centre. No turning back, for the bank I've left is no longer there, and the bank ahead seems so far away. The Weekend Bank. Beneath me the river of time moves, regardless of whether I make it to the Bank or not, not caring whether I slip and fall and disappear altogether. Time rushes past, a river in space, relentless. My past shoots back underneath me, the present churns up right beneath my feet, the future just beyond. No, I cannot look back. Monday has come and gone. So has Tuesday. It's Wednesday today. Two more days and then we have the Weekend.

So much to do – so much has been done. But always – so much is undone; not done; has to be done; tomorrow, the day after, the next week, the next month – will it never end? Let's see – this week – the children had to be taken to school, for ballet classes, swimming squads, tuition classes, piano lessons after school. They come home tired, wanting a drink, a sandwich, a snack, lunch, dinner. They have homework to do, they want to watch TV 'for just a minute longer' and I fold, crumple, and give in. I cannot argue with them, not anymore. I'm tired of saying 'don't' and 'stop' and 'it's time to do this or that'. Then they sleep. Like angels ensconced in the clouds of their pillows, Tiggers and Winnie the Poohs gaze wide eyed, while Barbie and Ken stand at the edge of the bed about to break into some incredible routine. My husband, spouse, beloved, Ron sleeps soundly, his face almost babylike while he snores softly. My eyes close as I drowsily drift and dream of faraway places - long curving roads, bridges that go on forever, of floating on snow clouds someplace high up. The alarm pierces my brain and I stretch out to kill it. Everyone is asleep. Ron beside me, the children in their beds, Tessie the dog on her cushion on the floor. All in dreamland, breathing softly, smiling or scowling in their sleepiness. I get up - first the bathroom, then the kettle. Tea, coffee, milk, breakfast, sandwiches for school, drink bottles to be filled. Have you washed? Have you got your books together? Have you, have you, have you? Ron is gulping his tea. A brief kiss and they go. I'm alone. The breakfast table is a garbage platter, full of dirty plates, dirty mugs, banana peels, bread crusts, dabs of butter. I sigh and reach out for the dishwash detergent. Floors to be swept, beds tidied, bathrooms washed. Clothes in the machine, humming along in their own sing song, spinning crazily, then dead stop. Clothes on the line. Clothes to be ironed. Clothes to be put away. Meals to be prepared, chopped, cut, cooked. The newspaper lies unfolded as I pass it a thousand times. Time to shower and change. Cool water runs down my body. I hear the telephone ring, the polite voice on the answering machine, my voice – then a soundless crackle and that's it. The water soothes, the water cools, the water calms. I stretch one leg toes pointed, then the other leg, feeling the tension of the muscles ripple through my skin. Arms up stretch stretch stretch – a piece of elastic drawn to its ultimate.

Snap! Back to now. I'm dressed. I check my list – those longwinded rigmaroles I write about - what I have to do, where I have to go, people I have to meet. Never ending. Every single day there's a new lot to be done. Old lots ticked off and crumpled into balls for the waste paper basket. I steady myself. Gather my thoughts. I have to get so much done before the Weekend. All the jottings have to be ticked off, crushed, thrown away. Done – completed.

Thursday comes and goes like it was never there. Never existed. Then Friday – the Bank is closer. Quite visible, really. I see the grass, tall and untrodden. The trees in the distance wave their branches, and brightly coloured flowers wink at me like lanterns in the night. I'll soon be there, I cry. But Friday is only beginning and it's still too far away for them to hear me.

Friday evening descends and my steps long to slow down, but unconsciously my feet gather speed. I am now running to get the things I haven't got done before I step ashore. My lists my lists -I have to check my lists, and tick them off. Done – completed. I have to put everything away, pack my bags, be ready to take the Saturday morning leap, before the bridge collapses under me.

As I jump I hear the snap of the ropes, and when I look back there is nothing, nothing except the roar of the river underneath. It's the Weekend at last. I flop into the long tall grass and look up at the trees. I listen to the birds chatter and the insects making their curious tik tik noises. Tessie barks and bounds up to me, and I hug her. We sit together, so close I can feel her breath on my face. The children are playing with Barbie and Ken who are getting married today. They're all dressed up for the wedding. Ron is fiddling with the car, the bonnet is open and he's talking to something inside there. I lie under a tree and close my eyes, the cascade of a waterfall somewhere tinkles like a wind-chime in my ear. I fall asleep and dream – but only for a while. The Weekend is crossed even quicker than I imagined.

Come Monday and I will be ready to step out again into another week. Into the unknown. And before I know what, it will be Wednesday again and there I'll be, doing my balancing act right in the middle of yet another suspension bridge.

Tuition Class

Latha picked up the two baskets, one overflowing with vegetables and the other with dry rations, and gazed wearily at the stairway before her. A stubborn determination belied her slight build as she strode up the steps with a basket in either hand and her handbag slung across her shoulder. How different from our place in Matara, she thought. I would never have to struggle up steps like this! Her husband Jayasiri worked for the Government and with his recent promotion to Chief Audit Clerk, a well earned reward for his hard work over the past five years, was transferred to Colombo. They were provided with accommodation in a block of government flats located in Kirullaponne, one of Colombo's suburbs.

As she entered their flat Latha's eyes were stinging, and, although she tried hard to dismiss it, her back did ache with the weight she had hauled upstairs. The flat had two minute bedrooms, bathroom, small hall and dining area, a narrow rectangular kitchen, all cramped within the confines of a tall concrete building. They were on the topmost floor, the fourth, and Latha bemoaned the fact that each time she went out marketing she had to carry her purchases up so many flights. The only 'garden' available was a minute square of dust with a stunted jam fruit tree at ground level, and she had to be satisfied with a few potted plants placed on the narrow balconies which flanked either side of the flat. Even this was not convenient as she had to dry the clothes in these areas as well, so she would constantly have to shift her beloved plants to create more space. She thought of her garden at home filled with trees of coconut, *jak* and other fruits, and a variety of flowers and foliage.

Jayasiri felt important and pleased with his new position in the office, for now he received a bigger income and could send his children to 'good' government schools in the big city. He also enjoyed the fact that he had to visit other government offices in connection with his auditing work. Sometimes he had to go out of Colombo to nearby towns and often had to work after regular office hours and even on a Saturday and Sunday. He was rewarded with overtime payments and planned to use the extra money for special things for his family, but soon realized that this was almost impossible, for in the urbanized corridors of Colombo even coconuts and *mallung kola* cost double the price from those in Matara. A man of silent disposition he was often found at home dressed in a sarong and banian seated on a chair reading a newspaper.

At first, Nandani who was nearly fifteen and twelve year old Saman, were thrilled to be 'living in the sky' as they called it. Nandani was tall for her age and fair like her mother, although she had her father's big eyes and curly hair. Saman was dark complexioned and of small build, still waiting for the spurt of teenage hormones to shoot him up some inches, and was a lively and energetic boy. They loved racing up and down the steps, then panting, they would lean over the balcony watching the clouds scud by. They would mimic the calls of the birds perched at eye level on the flamboyant trees across the road. After school they scrambled to be the first under the shower in their bathroom, to have the water tickling their bodies, unlike the well baths in their village. The only thing they did not like was going to school. For one thing they had to attend different schools now, as co-education was not practised in most of the Colombo schools. They would take the bus to school each morning and had made a few friends already, but found their schoolwork different from what they had done before. In Matara they had played games like volleyball and cricket, but here their schoolwork took most of their time.

Often Latha was summoned by the teachers and even the Principals to discuss their work.
"You will have to get them a tutor so that they can keep up with the others – otherwise they won't be able to do the government exams."
"I will have to discuss this with the children's father." was Latha's response, as she had never in all her married life taken a decision regarding her family without Jayasiri's advice.

Jayasiri came home late that evening – almost eight – soon after the children had finished their dinner and were getting ready for bed. He had his bath. He disliked the shower and filled a large bucket and poured water over his body with a small round bowl. He came out dressed in sarong and banian; Latha warmed the food and served some on a plate for him before she served herself. Jayasiri who had had only two *muspaans* for lunch ate with relish the rice, dhal, *haalmasso* curry and sambol that Latha had turned out. She mixed her food slowly with her fingers.
"Why? You're not hungry?" They asked.
"I'm quite worried."
"Worried? About what?"
"Today also I had to meet both Principals. The children's work is not so good. They said we will have to give them maths tuition. The English they can do at special classes in school."

Jayasiri ate silently.

Latha spoke again. "I thought of asking the next door lady – I see a tutor coming there every evening. She might know of someone. Don't know how much it'll cost."

"Don't worry about that, I'm earning well now, so that should be all right." After dinner, Jayasiri eagorly sat down to read the day's newspaper.

Next morning, after the children had left, Latha went over to meet her neighbour.

Mrs Rupasinghe opened the door, duster in hand and smiled when she saw Latha.

"Ah *kohomade* Latha – *hondate innawade?*" How are you - are you keeping well?

"Yes. I just wanted to ask you whether you can find a tutor for my two – they have English classes in school but I have to find someone for their maths - three times a week should do."

Mrs Rupasinghe nodded, "I can ask our tutor whether he knows anyone."

"How much would it cost?"

"Quite expensive now *aney*, about four or five hundred an hour. Anyway I'll let you know."

The following morning Latha was preparing the lunch when the doorbell rang.

She was surprised to see a stranger at the door. A fair complexioned man in his early thirties, of medium height with dark eyes under thick eyebrows, and short wavy hair stood there. He reminded her of a film star.

"I've come to ask about the tuition classes."

So this was the tutor.

Latha offered him a chair and sat opposite.

"The tutor who comes next door - Mr Galhena – told me about this. I give Maths tuition to children from the ages of ten to O level."

"Ah that's fine. Can you come three times a week – for both my children?"

He pulled out a diary and peered into it.

"What about Tuesday, Thursday and Saturday?"

"No Saturday is the only day we have at home, then we'll have it on two days to start with. Make it Tuesday and Thursday."

"Okay." He said making a note in his book.

"Will you have something to drink?"

"No – thanks – I'm in a hurry."

As he stood up to leave she asked him what his fees would be.

"I'll start with four hundred for both of them – we can see later."

"Alright." Latha's was relieved that he had quoted such a low rate.

After he'd left she realized to her dismay that she hadn't asked him anything about himself – not even his name!

Nandani and Saman were excited about the new tutor. By now they had grown tired of running up and down the stairs and found that the balconies were too hot during the day to stand and watch the clouds and the birds. In their dreams they ran through green paddy fields and splashed in the stream that flowed by their house; they saw their *aachchi* wash clothes at the well and their dog Chandi run around barking wildly. But when they awoke they discovered they had been bitten by mosquitos and suffered the stifling heat which only grew more intense as the day wore on. Their days were made up of the same routine - going to school, returning home, doing their homework, having their baths, eating their meals and going to bed.

They could hear the television blare from the adjoining flats but Jayasiri had refused to get one for them as he felt they would neglect their studies.

Tuesday 4 pm the bell rang and the tutor stood there briefcase in hand. Latha gave the dining table where they were to work another wipe down. Nandani and Saman stared at him, too shy to speak but at the same time eager to make friends.

He smiled at them. "Ah you must be Nandani and you Saman – I am Mr Galhena's friend Sunil. Let me have a look at your school books so I can see where I can help you." They brought him the books and sat on either side of him at the small square dining table.

He went through their work individually and then set them some exercises.

"Do you like a cup of tea?" asked Latha.

"Alright – thanks."

She made the tea and placed the cup and saucer by his hand. She noticed his muscular hands and thought he must be doing a lot of physical work. His fingers were long and tapering and had clean neat short nails. Mr Sunil, as the children called him, never missed a class and after two weeks Saman went all the way down stairs to see him off. He came racing upstairs quite breathless, and carrying a magazine in his hand.

"What's that?"

"Mr Sunil gave me a magazine – it's called 'Time.' he said it was a good magazine, even if I don't understand everything it's good to read. He had so many in his three wheeler – I hope he gives me another one next time. Here Nandani he said for you also to read it." Nandani looked at him and giggled.

69

"What do you mean 'his' three wheeler?" Latha asked.
"Why the one he comes in – that belongs to him."

The lessons each Tuesday and Thursday progressed without a flaw. Each day Sunil would come on time and the two children would sit at the dining table following his instructions and listening to him with great intent. They seemed to enjoy their class and continued chatting and laughing with him even after the lesson was over. Sometimes Latha would bring out a packet of biscuits and they would sit at the table and talk. At the end of the first term their math scores had soared, much to everyone's delight.

"Do they still need tuition?" Jayasiri asked when he looked at their reports.

There was a deathly silence. Latha spoke after a while, "We can't stop him now. I mean they should continue the classes in order to maintain their standard."

Nandani and Saman watched their father with a questioning look in their eyes.

"Ah – if you say so – let them continue with the lessons then."

One evening Latha was in the kitchen washing the pans when she heard Sunil preparing to leave. Saman came charging into the kitchen "*Aney Ammi*, Sunil Sir says if we like he can take us to Galle Face for a ride today."

"Oh don't be silly, Mr Sunil must be having so much to do, don't worry him like this." She tousled Saman's hair.

"No no really - I have no work now so I could take all of you to Galle Face – it's a nice place in the evening."

Jayasiri was out of town and seeing the eagerness in her children's eyes, Latha had no reason not to agree to Sunil's suggestion. Soon they were in the red three wheeler, whizzing off in the direction of the Galle Face Green. She had heard so much about this place – but had never been there. Dusk had fallen and there were crowds of people meandering on the large grounds. Palmyrah palms stood like sentries along the edge nearer the main Galle Road. On either sides of the grounds stood stalls strung with tiny lights, where a variety of food items were being sold - ice cream, roti, vadai, kadala, slices of fruit - Nandani and Saman ran from place to place rushing back to Latha and Sunil to tell them what they'd seen. They stared in awe at the kites and balloons sold by vendors. Sunil and Latha strolled in the cool breeze of the evening. Then Sunil bought slices of pineapple which they ate as they walked. For Saman and Nandani he bought ice cream cones.

This was like the carnival they had in Matara some years ago, thought Latha. Sunil was talking to Nandani and Saman and telling them about the place pointing in different directions as he spoke. He has such patience with the children, Latha noted, not like Jayasiri who never has time to talk to them. She sighed and glanced at her watch and was shocked to see that it was almost dinnertime. "It's very late – we should get back home." Latha cried.

"Why? Thaththa is not here – so we can get a little late." Nandani pouted.

Sunil's eyes met Latha's but he remained silent. Saman was running down to have a look at the sea. Latha felt uneasy. She should have been enjoying this moment, suddenly she wished Jayasiri was here – he should have been with them now. But he wasn't. She gazed at the sea reflecting the bright lights from the shore and again thought of the sea at her home down south. A sharp breeze made her feel chilly and she began walking towards the threewheeler.

Nandani and Saman knew they had to follow her and Sunil lagged behind. They were already inside when he climbed in and started the engine.

"Thank you for taking us to the Galle Face Green." Latha was surprised when Nandani spoke out so openly. But it was good of him to take us, she thought, these are places we never see and never seem to get a chance of visiting.

He smiled and mumbled something. He drove slowly through the lighted streets and when they reached their flat he waited silently while they stepped down. Latha looked into the threewheeler and said, "Sunil, thank you very much for taking us." She reached out to touch his hand but quickly drew back.

"Why don't you come up and have a drink with us? " Nandani suggested.

"*Aiyo* yes – come will you Sir!" Saman tugged at his shirt sleeve.

Sunil looked across at Latha. "No – it's too late – some other time okay?"

As they reached their flat the children ran onto the balcony and Latha followed them. Sunil was still seated in the vehicle. Nandani and Saman called out to him and he peered out and waved.

The following week Latha watched the clock on the dining room wall. Saman was getting his books ready for the tuition class. The familiar rattle made her walk to the balcony. Looking out she saw the red three wheeler outside. Sunil looked up. She moved away quickly and went into the kitchen. Saman ran to the door when the bell rang. Sunil greeted him and looking over his head nodded at Latha.

As they sat at the table for the tuition lesson, Sunil asked, "Where's Nandani?"

"She's got fever – I gave her some Panadols also but it is still quite high. I'll have to take her tomorrow to the doctor – there's no way of doing it now."

Sunil glanced at his watch "Why, I can take you now – Saman can also come – and we can get back for the tuition class."

Nandani lay on the bed looking pale and listless. Her eyes were closed. Sunil went up to her and placed the back of his hand on her neck. "Hmm – quite hot – her fever must be high. She should see a doctor straightaway".

Latha hurriedly went inside her room and changed her blouse and skirt; then she combed her hair carefully tying it in a knot at the back of her neck, grabbed her handbag and went outside. She helped Nandani down the stairs and into the vehicle. The roads were crowded and they had to weave their way through the traffic. When they reached the hospital Latha was distressed to see the crammed corridors.

"Don't worry - I'll wait for you" said Sunil. He showed them inside and waited until the doctor had seen Nandani. When they reached the flat he helped Nandani up the steps. He took her into the room and helped her to bed.

Latha was doling out the medicines. There were tablets for the fever and an antibiotic for her bad throat. Sunil poured out a glass of water and gave this to Nandani with the medicines.

"Now Nandani you go to sleep, don't worry about anything – we can do the tuition class another day."

Latha was looking over his shoulder – a few inches away from her. She turned quickly and walked back to the dining table where Saman was getting his books out for his lesson. Sunil ran his fingers through his hair and looked over Saman's work. He pondered over the pages and didn't speak until Saman did.

"Sunil Sir – is my work alright?"

"What? Ah yes – let's see." He hunched over the page.

Latha watched silently from the kitchen. "Sunil – let me get you a cup of tea." He glanced at her and nodded. She made the tea the way he liked it, with a lot of milk and two teaspoons of sugar, in a mug and not a cup. Very hot. She stirred it clinking the spoon as she brought it to the table. He glanced at her as she placed it beside his hand on the table.

"I hope Nandani will be alright." He sounded worried.

Latha bit her lip. "Oh yes – the fever will take some time to go down – but I'm sure she'll be okay."

He drank his tea slowly and then went on to look over Saman's work. By the time he left it was past six o'clock. "I'll just look in at Nandani" – he walked into the room as though he was a part of the family. It's almost as if he belongs here, Latha thought.

"Saman stay here with *akka*." Latha said, while she walked out with Sunil. Down the narrow stairway they went, Latha holding on to the bannister with Sunil at her side, like a couple going out together, she thought. At the door Latha stopped, "Sunil I want to thank you very much for helping me today, I was really worried about Nandani."

"Don't mention it. I'm happy I was of some help."

She watched him drive away.

After a few moments she walked upstairs slowly reflecting on the afternoon's incident.

Saman looked up as she walked in. "Is *thaththa* coming early today?"

"Why?"

"No – I just asked. He's never at home now – we never get to see him."

It was true – Jayasiri was hardly ever at home now, Latha reflected. He had many trips to outstation branches on his audit work and sometimes he had to stay overnight too.

Even while in office he would work late and return home after the children had gone to bed. Of course he was rewarded with plenty of overtime dues and this goes towards our needs, so I mustn't grumble, she thought.

The next morning Nandani didn't go to school even though her fever had subsided. She felt weak and tired and Latha thought she should rest for a few days. Jayasiri had returned late that night and was still asleep at 9 am. Latha had finished sweeping the flat and was gathering the clothes that had to be washed, when he awoke. She immediately put the clothes down and went to set out his breakfast. She had made some stringhoppers, for Jayasiri didn't like the urban habit of a bread and butter breakfast. Latha placed them and some fish curry and sambol on the table. He had washed and changed for office and was already seated. "Hurry up – I have to go soon." he said, glancing at the clock. He ate silently and she stood by the kitchen door ready to give him that really hot cup of tea that was in the making. Jayasiri gulped it down and left. She closed the door and heard his footsteps echo down the stairs. After he'd gone she realized she had forgotten to tell him about Nandani's fever. He comes so late and then rushes off – we have no time to even talk now. She sighed and went back to work in her small kitchen. Now the lunch had to be prepared. While she was scraping the coconut she heard the doorbell. She never had any visitors so she wondered who it could be at this time of the morning. Wiping her hands on a cloth she answered the door and was taken aback to see Sunil standing there with a bag in his hand.
"Why Sunil!"
"Ah – I was passing this way – here some oranges."

Latha could barely breathe. She took the bag of fruit and put them into the small 'fridge.

He was staring at her when she turned around. They sat opposite each other and Latha felt confused and didn't know what to say to him. Then she broke the awkward silence. "Will you have a cup of tea?"

"Yes, I'd like that."

He came and stood by the kitchen door as she brewed the tea and she could smell the scent of some cologne – something sweet and spicy.

"I have something to tell you Latha." He moved closer.

"Here your tea is ready, let's go out and sit." she said, not wanting to be confined in the small area of the kitchen with him where she could almost feel his breath and they would surely brush against each other in trying to move around.

She sat but he didn't. "What is it?" she asked, her words faltering.

"I have fallen in love, I think." Sunil whispered, looking down.

Latha gripped the handle of her mug and spoke slowly. "What do you mean you 'think'?" She gave a light laugh.

"Not 'think' I am sure." Now he looked directly at her.

She felt a tightening in her chest.

"Latha – I don't know how to tell you this."

Latha remained silent.

"I'm in love with Nandani." His words were inaudible.

"What?" she cried out.

He repeated himself. She felt herself falling through some deep dark tunnel where everything was racing along, her heart, her breathing, her whole body. She bent down holding her head in her hands.

"What's wrong – are you alright?" He said leaning forward.

She waved him away. "No - no! What nonsense is this?" her voice sounded strange to her, distant, cracked, shaking.

76

"I'm sorry – I felt I had to tell you. I am willing to wait till she's older."

"No ! what rubbish – she has to concentrate on her exams – she's far too young for this sort of thing."

"I'm really sorry I didn't think you - of all people - would disapprove so much. I don't know what to do." His eyes misted as he spoke.

"You are not to come here again, do you hear me? This is such nonsense. I can always find another tutor."

Sunil stood up and went to the door. "I'm sorry Latha that I have upset you, but I thought you knew about it. I thought you had sensed something between us and that you didn't mind. But now I know I was wrong. I'll leave – just tell Nandani I won't see her again. I won't be coming for the tuition classes anymore."

He left, shutting the door softly behind him. As she sat on the small two seater chair, she heard his footsteps echo down the stairway. Her eyes blurred and tears trickled down her face. How foolish I have been, thinking such silly thoughts. I'm a married woman and have a husband and family and what nonsense was going on in my head. But I can't let him have Nandani – it will be too much to deal with. I wish I had never met him. She took the oranges from the fridge and flung them into the bin.

"*Amma* did someone come? Was that Mister Sunil's voice I heard?" It was Nandani calling out to her.

She steeled herself and walked into the room. "Yes it was Sunil. He said he can't continue the classes as he has some other assignments to attend to."

Nandani sat up with a jerk. "What? He's not coming here again?"

"He's got another job– so he won't be coming."

77

The girl hugged the pillow against her and sobbed.
Latha went back to the kitchen and began scraping the coconut for lunch.

The End and the Beginning

Sepalika was putting her husband's clothes away in his cupboard - as she had done for the past thirty odd years - when the doorbell rang.

The shirts go in there, the sarongs one shelf below- who's that? Can't do a thing without being disturbed. The dogs began barking as Karuna answered the door. Sepalika heard a man's voice.

Karuna came panting to the room. "Missi – two policemen have come to meet you. Don't know why." Her voice was breathless.

Policemen? Now what? Sepalika dumped the clothes on the bed and rushed outside.

Karuna propped the broom against the wall and hovered nearby.

"Mrs Jayasinghe? "
"Yes."
"Madam – do you know who this is?" They showed her an ID card.

She peered at it "Yes yes – this is Mohan's ID – my husband -but -?"

The older of the two policemen spoke.

"Some bad news."

"What?"

"Your husband met with an accident- near Ambalangoda. A lorry was overtaking him and went right across the road – it crashed straight into his car." He paused, looking hard at her. "There was no chance at all."

Mohan had left for Galle early that morning. Oh God – now he was dead. Sepalika held her hand to her mouth and gasped.

Karuna rushed to her "Aney Missi – what happened?" She looked at the policemen.

"The Mahathaya - an accident –"

"Aiyo! What happened?" Karuna was wringing her hands.

"He died – would have been instantly."

Sepalika stood still, her hand covering her face. She moaned and shook her head.

"Give Madam some water to drink."

"Come Missi – come and sit –I'll bring some water. Aiyo what a thing to happen no!"

Sepalika heard Karuna giving the policeman her son's telephone number. In a blur she saw the policeman walking to the far side of the room, his phone pressed against his ear. Suddenly she felt quite light headed. The walls and the furniture were spinning and she too wanted to pirouette around the room. But someone gripped her by the arm and she felt herself being put on her bed.

She heard voices. Was that Ruwan – her beloved son? Karuna's voice – then someone else's – maybe the policemen. A door shut.

Ruwan sat by her bed clutching her hand. "Amma – it's so awful. Why did he have to die like this? I don't know what we are going to do without him." He put his head on her hand and she felt his tears.

She looked hard at Ruwan. No one would believe he was twenty eight years old; he looked like a little boy crying like that, sniffling into a handkerchief.

He left her to answer a tap on the door. The policeman and he were talking. Words drifted in.

"I don't think she should go to identify the body Officer – she's in a state of shock – I'll go."

She lifted herself from the bed. "I'll go with you Putha."

"No no – you stay– I can do it with Sita Aunty and Charlie Mama."

Sepalika clenched her fists. "No – let me go with you Ruwan – I want to." *I have to be sure, she thought.*

The morgue was a large boxy building with walls that had now taken on a mottled grey hue with large black patches where the damp had set in. Fluorescent strips, fitted high on the walls and cross beams, cast an eerie light on everything below.

Two men dressed in white coats led them inside.

Sepalika felt her knees shake and was relieved that Ruwan, Sita and Charlie were with her. Ruwan led her into the room. As she entered an icy draft made her draw her sari pota taut over her shoulders. A few feet away stood a cement slab with something on it, covered with a thick sheet. She cringed as she thought of Mohan's body lying on that slab.

The policemen stood by. One of the men in white stepped forward and drew the sheet down.

Even though she knew what to expect, the shock of it made Sepalika shudder. Sita placed her hand around her shoulder and drew her close. Ruwan let out a muffled cry and turned away.

The body on the slab was definitely Mohan. The unmistakable aquiline nose, full mouth and dark eyebrows were as unblemished as when she last saw him that fateful morning. He looked like he was asleep - not after an accident that had killed him. Sepalika glanced at the policemen with a puzzled look.

"He was knocked on the back of his head – severe concussion and probable instant death. Other than that he only has a few bruises - some broken ribs – and a smashed ankle."

On the way back home Ruwan sat holding her hand, staring out of the window, while she was still and silent.

Her sister and brother in law who were in front spoke in hushed tones.

"I want to lie down – rest a bit." Sepalika said when they reached the house.
"You rest – we'll see to everything – don't worry." Sita spoke as she led her into her room.
Sepalika fell into a restless sleep, and then awoke with a start. Only the whirring of the fan overhead broke the silence. Somewhere a clock struck – she didn't count – the chimes seemed to go on and on. Her thoughts were muddled and confused as she tried to recall the events of that day. Slowly they came back to her. Mohan had died in a car crash. It's not true – can't be. Why, only this morning he was here in this very room, and even though I didn't wake up when he left, I did hear him start the car and rev the engine before he took off. And now – now he was dead. How difficult to believe – but true. She raised herself on her elbows and sat up in bed. Her legs trembled as she rose and walked slowly in the dark, to the haansi putuwa by the window in their room. This was where Mohan always sat and read the newspapers. His chair. Gently she lowered herself onto it and made herself comfortable. It was not his chair anymore. Now she could use it whenever she wished. The window was open and she could hear the staccato tunes of the night insects. Her hands shook as she cupped them together over her mouth and tried to say something aloud - to herself. But the words stuck in her throat- like one of those sharp fish bones.

The click of the door handle made her open her eyes for she had fallen asleep on the chair. The soft hues of a new day stole in through the curtains.
"Amma – you're up." Ruwan came to her. His eyes were red and bleary and he held a large white handkerchief

against his face. She felt sorry for the boy – he doted on his father so. It was a hard blow for him.

She felt an arm go round her shoulders. When she looked up it was the face of her younger sister Sita. Her small face looked pinched and her eyes were red.

"Nangi, I can't believe that Mohan is dead. I don't remember what happened to me yesterday – after I spoke to those two policemen." She grasped Sita's hand.

"You almost fainted when you heard the news– then Ruwan called us and I stayed over – and then we had to go to the morgue." Sita looked down. "Charlie is busy with the funeral arrangements, we'll do everything- you mustn't worry about anything." She stroked Sepalika's head.

Karuna came into the room. "Here *Missi* –a cup of tea for you." She stood by the bed and stared at Sepalika. "*Mahaththaya* should have taken Gunadasa no, to drive the car – just in vain he went by himself."

She ignored Karuna's remark. "Leave the tea Karuna – I'll drink it later –I don't like it hot."

As she lay back and closed her eyes, she heard Sita's voice "I'm sorry akka is resting - she's in a terrible state of shock, it was all so sudden."

Other voices -"Yes so terrible for her – and the boy. Just tell her that we came. We'll come later and see her."

"It'll take some time for her to get over it."

"When is the funeral?"

"This evening. 4.30 from here."

"Poor thing!"

Voices – so many voices, dinning into her head.

She remained seated, her head buzzing. She shivered trying to shake off the strong sense of claustrophobia she felt.

Her thoughts were interrupted by Karuna's voice – " Missi better have a wash and start dressing –for the funeral – in a little while the priest will come."
I can't believe that so much time had gone by since the accident. When was it? Yesterday? The day before? Minutes, hours, days had blurred into a timeless phase, for Sepalika had not left her room since her visit to the morgue.
Well, I'll have to dress up now for the funeral. She had a shower and wore a white sari that Sita had put out for her. Sita helped her dress, her eyes serious, her hands gentle and comforting.

"Akka, the priest is here."
Sepalika went out and met the priest from the local church. The tall elderly man in white robes clasped her hands. "I was so sorry to hear about Mohan. It must be such a shock for you. May God give you the strength you need at this time. I tried to see you yesterday but you were resting."
"Yes - a terrible shock. I feel so – " she pursed her lips and shrugged.
"I know what a loss it is." He eyed her with great compassion. She looked down saying nothing.

Crowds filled the house. There were friends and relations, but mostly there were Mohan's business associates. *How many times will I have to shake hands and stick my cheek out to be kissed and say thank you thank you thank you? I wish I could just get this over with – a fast as possible.* Sepalika wanted was to be left alone – to compose her thoughts. She was kicking and screaming inside, struggling to deal with the feelings that were coursing through her mind and body.

She sat by the coffin, averting her face as she didn't want to see him. But finally she had to look. There he lay, hands clasped together, silent and still. Mohan. Dead. She turned away quickly.

They sang hymns and repeated prayers which sent her into a kind of floating feeling. Everything seemed to drag on and on, making her feel exhausted. Finally the time had come to close the coffin. She stood still knowing that everyone expected her to kiss Mohan at this moment. *I can't do it – I really can't.* Then Ruwan guided her forward until she was leaning against the coffin, she could feel the smoothness of the wood and the silk tassels. The scent of roses and carnations filled her nostrils. Someone had sprayed scented cologne – a flowery fragrance and the combination of odours made her feel dizzy. But she knew she had to do it. Closing her eyes she forced herself to bend down and press her lips on Mohan's forehead. The icy cold touch of his skin made her draw back sharply. She stepped aside quickly wishing she could just go back home and forget about all this. But no, there was so much more to be done. They got into their cars and followed the hearse to the cemetery. Once there they walked behind the hearse right up to the burial grounds. Sita and Ruwan stood with her. She looked down and closed her eyes.
The coffin was carried to the gravesite and placed on a steel frame with belts attached to it. More hymns, more prayers. Sepalika felt faint. Wasn't this ever going to end, she wondered.
The priest intoned.
"Earth to earth, dust to dust – ashes to ashes –"
Someone nudged her. She stepped forward, picked up a fistful of earth and tossed in into the grave. *Earth to earth, dust to dust, ashes to ashes.* She gazed at the coffin being

lowered into the rectangular opening in the ground. The wide belts supporting it creaked and groaned as they unraveled. "Amazing Grace how sweet thou art "–the singing soared up into the trees. Her head began to throb and she longed to get back home.

Friends and relations gathered at the house after the funeral, as was the custom. The clatter of plates and cutlery meant that dinner was being served. Figures moved up and down, some stopped and said something to her. Some even sat down beside her and held her hand as they spoke. *I wish I could just go to my room.* Sita brought her a plate filled with rice, dhal curry, dried fish cooked in a spicy gravy, –"Here akka some food. You must eat no - you'll feel better. "
Silently, Sepalika took the plate. *It's too much*, she wanted to say, but knew they would insist that she should eat it all. Sita sat by her.
After a few mouthfuls she spoke. "I don't feel like eating Nangi, I just want to lie down – a slight headache." A hand encircled her waist and led her towards her bedroom.
"Amma, are you okay? " Ruwan had already asked her this a thousand times.
"Yes – yes I'm alright."

She closed the door and stood by the bed, absorbed in the silence within the room. *At last I can be by myself –so many things to sort out.* She recalled that fateful morning – the day Mohan died. He was going to Galle, on work, he said. Then she remembered the telephone conversation she had overheard the night before.
"Yes yes – I'll come tomorrow. No she won't know." He laughed – not the derisive one he used for her, but a giggle. Like a schoolboy playing truant. " I'll come in time for breakfast."

86

That's all she needed to know.

Over the years she had ignored the conversations that stopped short when she entered a circle of people, or the overheard whisperings that fluttered against her ears. But at night they rose from the deep recesses of her mind and drummed into her head until it throbbed, making it impossible for her to sleep. A surge of anger built up and she would vow to deal with him the next day. But when dawn broke, the anger dissolved into fear and shame – fear of losing her son and shame that would be brought on the family - and her vow disappeared into the humdrum of the waking day.

But that was all in the past. Everything had changed now.

She couldn't remember when she had last sat at her dressing table. Slowly she undid her *konde* and her hair fell way past her shoulders. Streaks of white showed here and there but it was still thick and wavy. As she brushed her hair she felt she was looking at another person. Her eye caught the reflection of the bed in the mirror. Now it was her bed. Its expansive width seemed a luxury to her. Her eyes burned when she remembered Mohan sleeping there, flat out after a drunken night. Hands flung carelessly, mouth open, snoring loud. How often she had to keep awake for the slam of a car door, the front door and then watch with half closed eyes as Mohan stumbled into bed. Even worse were the times when she would wait up, fall into a troubled sleep, only to find upon waking up in the morning that Mohan had not come at all. Then she would have to invent all kinds of excuses for the servants and her son the next morning. *I won't have to do any of this anymore. Never, ever again.*

On a hot muggy day three weeks later Sepalika opened her almirah and looked long and hard at the clothes hanging there. All grey, white, or blue. The clothes folded on the shelves were the same colour. This has been the colour of all my married life, she thought. Mostly greys and whites. I had to dress modestly to please my husband, please his family. Perhaps a little red or orange when Ruwan was born. But that soon faded away. Mohan sent Ruwan to his old school, made him play the games he had played, saw to it that he did Business Management and Accountancy to follow in his own footsteps. When Sepalika tried to take him to art classes, Mohan had protested so loudly that the boy refused to go. When Sepalika wanted him to learn the piano, which he was fond of and often tried the one at home, Mohan scoffed that "music lessons were only for girls and sissies" and promptly sold the piano even though she had begged of him to keep it. "I don't want you to put any silly notions into my son's head, piano lessons, what rubbish!" – he had screamed.

She sat on the edge of the bed and sighed. Reaching out, she touched the empty space on the bed savouring the soft smoothness of the sheets. *Gone*, she said in her head, then whispering – "Gone gone gone!" She looked around the room. The dark heavy cupboards, the flower patterned carpet, the four poster bed – everything reminded her of Mohan. *I want to get rid of them – sell them off and get some new furniture, stuff I like.* Her whole being was filled with a strange sensation. The muscles in her body became slack, her limbs loose and languid. When she stretched she seemed to reach out forever. *There are so many things I want to do – so many things I could never do before.* She lay down, hugged a pillow and closed her eyes.

Tomorrow was a new day in her life.

THE BEGINNING:

She walked to the window and drew the curtains. The sound of birdcall caught her ears. The darkness of the night had been dispelled with the new day. Suddenly she felt as if a heavy cloak had fallen off her shoulders. The past burdens of obedience, duties, traditions, customs – all these seemed to disappear. Now she could wear a mantle of gossamer – and fly as high as she wished.

Mirror Reflections

It was Rohan's sixtieth birthday party and the visitors had begun to arrive. Helen enjoyed her role of hostess. She mingled with the guests, seeing that they had their drinks, and all those delectable eats she had ordered, introducing them to one another, stopping every now and then at the little groups to join in the conversation. Suddenly she saw Dilani and Jehan – they were standing in the hallway, looking around, trying to spot a familiar face in the crowd. She was walking across the room to meet them when she spotted herself in the mirror on the wall. It was a large oval mirror, one that belonged to her mother. The frame was made of jak and the intricate grain of its wood stood out beneath the polish.

She was close to the mirror's shiny surface now. A face looked back. The angular lines and high cheekbones were now softened with the padding of forty years. The nose was still sharp and the brown eyes still sparkled. She looked hard at herself. No, the odd grey bits were still not noticeable. Her shoulder length hair was still thick and flicked out at the ends – a fashion which had come around again, as fashions always do. Fashions come and fashions go, she mused, only I just go on – I can't come back, ever.

She sighed as she recalled that twenty years ago a different face had looked back at her. Olive skin, smooth complexion, sharp nose, large brown eyes, curved mouth. A neck smooth and swanlike and shoulders that curved gently. Glossy brown hair shone in the reflection of the lights that played on the mirror. A glitter in her eyes that could only be matched by the stars or the flash of a diamond. The diamond on the ring on her finger placed there by Rohan. She looked down at the ring and the figure in the reflection did the same. Sparkles burst from it – the same way she felt about Rohan. Sparkly. She smiled and glanced up and her image responded.

Twenty years before, a young girl was tearfully scrutinizing herself in this very mirror. She turned her face this way and that, examining the spot on her forehead and cursing herself. What do I do? I have to look good for this evening. The eyes welled with angry tears and the mouth stood grim and hard. She adjusted her hair, tied back in a pony tail. Should I have it loose or tied up? This hairstyle is so – so childish. Again she cursed – nothing in particular, but everything in general. Damn – what should I do?

And then there was a time when a little girl stood there. She had to climb onto a stool so she could have a better look for the mirror was placed too high. The face was clear and the large brown eyes twinkled. The mouth soft and the cherubic contours glowed with vitality – an angelic face some said. The sleek angular bones were hiding behind the chubby cheeks which dimpled when she smiled. Hi -- she said in a high pitch voice and the face in the mirror replied. She giggled as she leapt off the stool.

She wondered – twenty years from now? The grey hair would show – but not if she took to dyeing it like most of her friends did. Would it be long, tied at the nape of her neck in a bun, or short and swept back from her face. Would the firm neck sag and the determined chin sink into rounded tranquility? Would there be furrows on that clear brow and creases stretching outwards from the eyes – would the neck hang in folds and the shoulders slacken?

Or perhaps there would be no image at all, for in twenty years who could say whether even she would be there!

A touch on her shoulder shook her out of her reverie.
"Oh Dilani and Jehan – how very lovely to see you. Come come – have something to drink."

Without even a glance at the mirror she moved away. The reflection disappeared, tucked away in some corner waiting to make its appearance again.

The Get-together

Ever since they left school, the four of them vowed to meet as often as possible. At the beginning they met every year, but as time went on other responsibilities crept into their lives and they lost touch with one another. And now, over a decade later, here they were at the Golden Dragon, meeting together for lunch.

Ruwani went hot and cold when she got the telephone call from Andrea telling her about it. It'll be so good to meet up with the old crowd again - after all they are my oldest friends, she recalled fondly. We used to have such fun together. I can't wait to meet them and give them all the news.

Charlene and Andrea were always in the fashion pages and will probably be dressed to kill. Even in school they always wore the latest fashions and had a host of admirers. I'd better wear something nice or I'll look a rag bag next to them. Ruwani went through her wardrobe and finally decided on a blue trouser and blouse to match. Better not wear a tee shirt - too casual. Placing the clothes against her, she scrutinized her reflection. How I wish I were tall and slim - such a curse being short and plump. Frowning at the unruly curly mop on her head, she brushed her hair down hard trying to keep it in place. It has to look good- at least for today. There - I don't look too bad, she thought, as her mouth broke into a wide smile showing a set of white but uneven teeth, and her bright small eyes twinkled.

Charlene and Andrea were there when she arrived. They were seated at table facing the window, pouring over the menu. She heard them when they spotted her.

"There's Ru." they said and looked at each other and smiled.

"My Ru you haven't changed at all except that you've cut your hair - looks much nicer than your long hair - that used to look quite wild, flying all over." said Andrea. Ruwani cringed, knowing that her hairstyle had always been one of convenience and not of fashion. They hugged her, careful not to get their lipstick smudged or their hairstyles disturbed, and she breathed in the expensive perfumes that came from their necks and arms.

Andrea wore a short navy dress, her trim figure and well groomed appearance made her look like a model. Charlene was a fusion of beige, with jewellery to match -a perfect piece of sculpture. Ruwani tugged at her sleeveless cotton blouse, pulling it down to cover her flabby abs. That's the word, not 'stomach' but abs. Tighten your abs, the advertisements said. She drew in her abs.

"Ah here comes Chandra. My, how fat she's become!"Charlene put the menu aside and stared at her. Chandra wore a pair of wide bottomed pants and flower pattered blouse and was bedecked in gold. Earrings, chains and bangles jingled and shone on her hands. Jingle jangle like the Perahera elephants, Ru thought.

"Sorry I'm late," said Chandra, "but I had to organise the children's lunch - don't you know? So difficult to get a good servant these days no, I have to tell them exactly what to make otherwise they do some nonsense *aney*. My kids are very fussy about their food - and I had to rush to the supermarket to get the French fries for them."

94

"I just give mine money- so I have no problem with their lunch." said Charlene.

Ruwani had no children, no lunch problems.

Andrea took a deep breath and spoke. "I'm of course taking a course in cake making - I want to plan what I'll do when the children leave for university – long time more I know – but one has to be focussed, otherwise once they go, life becomes hell!" She sighed heavily.

The idea of children walking out of the door and the demons of hell attacking Andrea and her husband make Ruwani giggle.

"Ru you can laugh - you have no responsibilities, nothing to worry about."

Charlene said "I'm glad I'm working, I don't know how anyone can stay at home - it's so boring."She glanced almost accusingly at the others.

"I'm of course really busy, involved in all kinds of charities, all *kinds* of charities," Chandra twisted her mouth and threw up her hands as she spoke. She always used to do that, Ruwani thought. In school she did it when she wanted to spite someone.

"My husband is always away on work, so I get bored *aney*. How much to watch videos - I have seen all the new movies. And then of course I go for my keep fit class to the Hilton twice a week."Andrea's whining tone had intensified over the years.

That's what I should be doing. Keep fit classes.

"I need a break from my husband and family- too much stress, I'm going to Singapore for a few weeks." Chandra announced. All eyes were riveted on her. "Anyway, I have to get some new kits also -must do some proper shopping once in a way no?"

They ordered the food after they'd discussed the menu at length. Sipping lime juice they waited for the food. Finally it arrived - vegetable fried rice, cuttlefish in butter sauce, sweet and sour chicken, kankung beef, prawns in batter, and vegetable chow mein.

They chatted while they ate.

Andrea looked at Ruwani. "You're so quiet. So- what have you been up to?"

"Oh - all kinds of things- and also -." I really should tell them about my writing - and Nalin.

"What kind of things? You must do something with yourself no - go out and meet people - otherwise how can you meet someone?" Charlene's face creased in abject sympathy.

"I write." The words rushed out.

"Write? What do you write about?"

She takes a deep breath. "Oh -articles, stories - some poetry."

"Poetry? For what?"

"Because I like to."

The clatter of cutlery broke through the silence that followed.

"You must take yourself in hand Ru."

Ru smiled. Such a lovely phrase, she thinks, 'take yourself in hand' - she pictures herself bending over and scooping her body up in her hand - there was she sitting in her very own hand! Weird.

They stare at her.

Dessert comes. Everyone has ordered something different.

Ruwani ate her fruit salad and stirred her ice cream until it melted into milk. I should tell them about Nalin. She glanced at the thin gold band on her finger. They haven't even noticed, she winced.

"You must do something with your life - you can't go on drifting like this."

"I must tell you that -"she begins.

"Do you still do that magazine work from home?"Chandra screwed up her nose.

"Yes." She paused for a moment. "Also I got -" Ru starts again, playing with her dessert spoon.

"You mustn't let yourself go." that was Charlene giving her the once over.

"You must do some exercises to get your abs down - why don't you buy one of those machines they advertise on TV - the Hilton is good but quite expensive."

I should have got my abs in shape before this get together Gosh this is awful - I have to escape. The loo - the best escape place in a restaurant.

"'Scuse me - " she got up, catching their whispered chatter as she was leaving.

"Poor thing - no wonder she's not settled - how can she, when she's stuck at home the whole day?"

"I don't know what she does - writing the whole time. So boring."

Ruwani sat on the toilet seat, put her head in her hands and sighed. What the hell am I doing here? Are these the friends I had in school? They've changed so much- or have I changed? Everything's so - so different. Her eyes stung. Then on a sudden impulse she decided. What the heck I'm quite happy as I am - I'll just go out and face them - who cares what they think anyway?

She made her way back to the table. Their heads were bent low and they were carrying on a muffled conversation, while peering out of the window.

"Myee Ru - you missed a super sight no. The most handsome hulk walked past the window - we thought he was coming in, but he looked hard at us and went right past." Charlene spoke, her eyes blinking, lashes fluttering until they almost popped out. They craned their necks to get a better view of the street outside, squealing like a chorus of mice. Ru sat backing the roadway and she definitely wasn't going to turn around to peek. This is what we used to do in school, giggling over some guy walking on the street. But at thirty-five? It's lunatic.

"Haven't seen anyone so handsome *aney,* he makes me feel funny all over." More giggles. Ruwani sighed. Maybe this is what happens when you have husbands like theirs. She'd seen their pictures often in the local newspapers and magazines. Smug bug types - big business and all that-slick haired, some already potbellied, impeccably clad - success scrawled all over their faces.

Charlene got up and went outside 'just to see' she said. She came back twisting her bum and walking with one foot in front of the other like a model on the catwalk. Ru stared at her, what the hell's happening?

"Myee- was he there?"

"Useless men - he has disappeared."

"Must've got scared when he saw us - I'm sure he wanted to come in here. Don't know what happened." More twitters.

They continue eating their desserts.

"So Ru say something will you?"

She cleared her throat. Now or never, she thought. "I got married."

Everyone at the table stops eating. They stare open mouthed and goggle eyed.

"What?" The high pitch could've cracked the glass.

"I got married."

"Married? To whom?"

"Nalin —"

"Nalin? Who's that?"

"The chap I married."

98

Silence. They cast sly glances at one another.

"So what does this, this Nalin chap do?"

"He's a chef - ."

"Oh."

"A chef?"

"Hmm."

Silence.

"Fine one you are Ru - to get married without telling us. So when was the wedding?"

"About two months ago."

They can't take their eyes off her. Then they chuckle. "Ah ha - newly weds."

"So where was it?"

"It was a quiet wedding- just a church affair -no reception."

"Is he - is he handsome?" Giggles.

"Hmm - he's cute." Ru feels her neck tingle and knows a blush is working itself up her face.

"Pity - maybe we could've fixed you up with Mr Gorgeous who just passed by - now it's too late -too late. You've missed the bus!"They throw back their heads and laugh.

They look like those Australian birds in the zoo - Laughing Jackasses they're called - opened their beaks and screeched non-stop. This is all too much for me.

A stifled silence follows as they concentrate on their meal, picking and choosing, munching and crunching. In between, they nudge each other and stare at the glass window just in case Mr Gorgeous - as they describe him- passes by. Ruwani watches them, squirming in her seat. I hope he doesn't pass again -God knows what they'll do. He'll think we're crazy- all of us. She realised that she was also part of the group and whatever they did would include her.

"Ru - why don't you take a look men - ?"

"Look will you- just get up and take a walk and look!"

"No I don't want to - I'm just - just not interested." she felt her face burn.

They snort "Ah, now she's a married woman -so she won't look."

I must get away from here. Ru glanced at her watch. "Do you mind -I have to leave soon - maybe we should call for the bill?"

Charlene put up her hand when the bill arrived and they tried to pay individually.

"*Aiyo* what's that men - this is on me. It's nothing. Sarath is making enough and this is just peanuts." She pulled out a few thousand rupee notes from her bag and placed them on the table.

"You can keep the balance okay." she looks up and dazzles the waiter with a toothy smile. He grins in return.

Chandra sighs. "Lot of packing to do *aney*, we are going to Nuwara Eliya tomorrow to see our horses race."

For a while they talk about the horse races.

Ruwani got up."I must call Nalin - he's coming to collect me."

"Ah then we can all get a good look at him." they giggle.

Won't they ever stop giggling? Ru groaned.

"Here Ru - you can use my cell phone men - no use of walking to the booth."

But she's already left. She feels their piercing eyes and cannot help but hear their loud whispers as she walks away.

"My - what a shock no - imagine Ru married!"

"Never thought anyone would marry Ru- she's so - so - quiet"

"What d'you think he looks like?"

"Who knows!"

They watch Ru at the 'phone booth across the room. Suddenly she swings around and smiles. Then to their astonishment they see this tall, well built, dark eyed- Mr Gorgeous himself- walking in towards them. They straighten themselves and gaze at him. But what's this? He's heading towards Ru, who's now returning to the table. She says something to them, but they are too stunned to listen. Words float over their heads, through them – "This is my husband Nalin – thanks for ----" Nothing but the beginning of the sentence enters their heads. Husband, Nalin, Mr Gorgeous – impossible! But there they are, Ru and Nalin, gazing into each other's eyes, laughing at God knows what. Like three petrified statues stuck to their chairs the others watch as Ru jauntily walks away, arm in arm with her Nalin.

Shut-Ins

Jeannie gazed at him seated on the old *haansi putuwa* on the verandah. Sarath looked older than his fifty one years. After the stroke he suffered his speech became a series of mumbles and grunts and he could use only his left hand. Being a natural right-hander this made it almost impossible for him to do simple things like eating or combing his hair or writing. His left leg had lost its life and he dragged himself along with the aid of a walking stick. Sitting on the curved armchair made him feel better even though it was not as comfortable as his wheelchair. He loathed the wheelchair, the chair for invalids. He loathed the word invalid, disabled, shut-ins. Even she winced whenever she heard people describe Sarath in this way. Made him sound useless. It hurt her to acknowledge that the description was really the truth. He was useless in a lot of ways and very much dependent on her, making her feel as shut in as he did.

She walked to the edge of the small garden and stood at the gate looking at the road which she had used so often; she remembered how sometimes it was a path of drudgery, especially when she had to carry heavy bags of vegetables and groceries. Now the road had taken on a different look. It looked inviting and seemed to beckon her outside. She recalled their early morning walks, when they stepped into a hazy kind of world before the sun was really quite awake and only the street lights glowed. He walked briskly, not pausing for even a second; she used to call him a robot. She always lagged behind never able to catch up with his express pace. Now look at him, she thought. His body drooped on the chair, one hand moved up and down to his face and onto the arm of the chair repeatedly. His mouth sagged to a side and sometimes unknown to him the spittle drooled onto his clothes. He would sit there, his shirt wet with saliva and then she would see it and wipe his mouth gently.

Jeannie returned quietly to the house. Every item of furniture was imprinted in her head as never before. The carved chairs in the drawing room and the old rectangular dining table with its heavy chairs looked dark and forbidding. She remembered how she used to polish the furniture until it gleamed. She remembered how she loved to cook, how he too loved to cook. They would often stand together in the well lighted kitchen and enjoy making favourite dishes like Thai Fried rice or Buhari chicken. They dared to venture into Italian foods and French recipes. The international cooks, they called themselves laughingly. Food took on a different role now. Everything he ate had to be pureed and mashed, soupy sloppy stuff that slid down his throat easily.

Her friends told her she should go out sometimes. It was easy to say, but who would stay with him? The daily help Seela wouldn't know what to do with him. When it happened, Seela was afraid even to look at him. She couldn't believe her master, the gentleman she had worked for the past so many years, had changed so much in an instant. She peered at him when he was brought back from the hospital on a wheelchair, unable to move unable to speak. Jeannie had to have an attendant to care for him during the day, but Sarath hated this strange man doing things for him. He wanted Jeannie by his side. In a month or two she asked the attendant to leave as he served no purpose in this house. She had to manage with Seela.

Two weeks ago she had received an invitation to a wedding. Sushila was an old school friend of hers and had called her, "Jeannie please try to make it to Choolie's wedding. I know it's difficult , but do try, we'll be so happy to see you." Jeannie noted the invitation was addressed to "Mr and Mrs Sarath Gooneratne." She turned down all the invitations now as it was so complicated to go out in the evenings. At least during the day she could dash out to the shops with Seela there at home to keep an eye on him. But in the evenings she was compelled to stay in.

When she showed the invitation to him he read it carefully and she knew he was looking at the time printed on it – '7 pm onwards.' He feared those times. It was as if a net had been cast over him which drew her in as well, but after Sushila's call she decided to accept the invitation. She had known Choolie as a baby and felt obliged to attend her wedding. Surely he wouldn't mind her going out just this once?
"I have asked malli to come and stay with you while I go to the wedding." She said.
He just stared at her, his face devoid of expression.

She was strangely excited about the wedding. Before, she avoided weddings, saying they bored her and she hated dressing up, and it was a waste of time. But now, it had become a real outing for her, almost an adventure. Which sari should she wear, the pink or the grey silk? She stood in front of her long mirror and put them against her, her eyes brightening at the thought of wearing these fineries and stepping into the outside world. She rummaged through her box of jewellery and picked up the amethyst earrings and ring to match. Now she had to find a suitable bracelet to wear. A smile played on her lips as she recalled the many times she had gone through these pieces, trying to match them with what she was wearing. But that was so long ago. The past ten months seemed like a lifetime.

Carefully, she ironed the sari and the jacket and the underskirt and hung them up in her bedroom. What if he wanted something while she was away? Would her brother understand what he said? Even she found it difficult to understand him sometimes. The water surged over her body while she showered. She sprayed herself with imported cologne and was dismayed to find that most of it had evaporated. Well never mind, she thought, I'll use what's left.

Her make-up had turned brittle and dry and was impossible to use. But she had a smooth skin and eyes that hadn't entirely lost their sparkle, and didn't need too much colour on her face. She combed her long hair and then pinned it up in a knot on the top of her head. He used to like that so much. How he used to watch her dress, telling her what jewellery to wear, admiring her outfit, laughing at her when her hair didn't say up perfectly. Suppose he had another stroke while she was away? After all that's what happened last time. She went out for a few hours to buy the groceries and when she returned he was slumped over his chair. She glanced at him. He was lying inert on the bed his eyes glued on her. He tried to smile but his mouth took on a grotesque shape which made her shudder. He said something but the sounds came out as a series of grunts which she could not understand. He was waving his left hand, calling her to his side. As she sat beside him he moved his hand across her face, touching it gently, trembling fingers playing on her ears and then he gripped her hand in his. A tear trickled down his numb face, making her turn away.

The doorbell rang. It was her brother Sugath. She went to the door and he was taken aback to see her eyes full of tears.

"What's the matter?" he asked.

"Nothing. I'm not going."

"But why? You're all dressed up and looking so pretty."

"No, I can't, it's just –"

"Is he telling you not to?"

"Oh no! I just don't want to go. I can't leave him. I know I should go but I can't." she sobbed.

He remained silent. "Don't worry, I'll sit with him and get him whatever he wants while you're away."

She shook her head. "No really, I'd rather stay at home, with him."

Sugath stood at the door and then said, "Okay – if that's what you want." He didn't attempt to come inside. "I'll come another time, maybe tomorrow, to see you both."

He left. She shut the door and leaned against it for a few moments, composing herself before she went back to the room.

Sarath gazed at her, eyes filled with anxiety expecting her to leave at any moment. She could see he was surprised when she slowly began undoing her jewellery and unwinding her sari. He tried to say something but the only sound that escaped his distorted lips was a series of agitated mumbles. He waved his hand frantically, calling her.

She sat by him on the bed. "My brother couldn't stay, he had some urgent work to attend to. It doesn't matter, I won't go. I really wasn't too keen on going anyway, you know how I hate weddings and dolling up." she gave a laugh which to her ears sounded hollow. She hoped her lie didn't sound the same.

But he looked happy. His mouth drooped in a contraption of a smile and saliva dribbled down his chin. She wiped his chin and held his hand and he gripped hers with a fierce tenderness that surprised her. In a curious way she felt relieved and happy she had stayed behind.

Rainburst

Anushka dozed off on a deck chair under the araliya tree. The book she was reading had fallen onto her lap, the point at which she had stopped hidden between its covers. Her hands dangled under the arms of the chair, fingernails blushing a pale pink, gently touched the grass. Her delicate mouth and eyelids fluttered as her chest rose up and down in gentle rhythm. The olive green pants and lollipop pink tee shirt she wore looked a part of the landscape – an exotic flower.

Her golden cocker spaniel Julie slept just a few inches away from the chair. Lying on her back, paws suspended in mid air, the dog sent out croaky snores. A ginger and white cat sat on the six foot high brick wall and gazed with narrowed eyes at the dog– his enemy- the beast that barked itself mad each time she saw him in the garden. Ginger and white sat still, flicking his tail. Oh to tear out the golden one's eyes right out of their sockets! Forget it – it's impossible. He gave a deep pussycat sigh from deep inside his chest, bristled his whiskers and began preening himself. Soon he was lost in the hypnotic rhythm of drawing his coarse tongue through the fur on his body.

The araliya tree stood like a giant canopy over the chair. Its firm green leaves glistening with dappled sunlight, its five petalled blossoms hung delicately in bouquets. Two straggly looking crows cawed raucously over a fish bone. A family of squirrels raced tails up, screeching, along the branch directly above Anushka, almost thirty feet above the ground. A white araliya gently loosened itself from its stem and fluttered down, landing softly on Anushka's hand.

It seemed as if she were holding the flower between her long slim fingers.

Next door, the neighbours argued.
"Don't put the clothes in the front garden, put them at the back."
"But the sun's in front!"
"It looks awful having clothes drying in the front garden."
"But that's where the sun-"
"I know I know, but it still looks horrid."
"They won't dry in the back garden."
"Put them anywhere then – make this look like a laundry – who the hell cares."
A door banged muffling the voices.

The twin boys from down the road were trying to fly a kite outside the wall of Anushka's house. There they ran, like double vision objects.
"Hang on, you fool – I'll hold one end and run with it and then you run behind me."
"No – I'll run backwards and you hold the damn kite and run towards me."
Their thudding footsteps crunched on the gravel road. Up and down they ran holding the kite and looking up as if something would come down and lift it up. And indeed something did. Quite unexpectedly a wind rose and with hardly any warning, lifted the kite, swishing it this way and that.
"Let the string roll – let it roll –"
As the stick-roll of twine unraveled at lightening speed the blue and red kite sauntered up into the sky, where it stood steadily for seconds then darted around having a game all on its own. The boys burst into shouts and danced along the

road as the kite bobbed high in the clouds a hundred feet above them.

In a house not too far away, a young man – short haired, wide eyed and firm mouthed – sat at a table in his room. He had a sheet of paper in front of him, and in his hand a pen stood poised waiting – waiting for the proper, no, the perfect words. With a sudden movement he began to write, with such fervour and passion, making faint tears on the paper with his eager scratchings. For the last time, he read it over. Yes, it sounded good. His eyes were blinded to the crumpled paper balls lying on the floor beside him. Folding the letter into four he wrote a name on the outside – Anushka, and sealed it with a kiss. Then he ran outside, leapt on his rusty bike and rode into the wind. Two boys were standing right in the middle on the road, gazing upwards and pulling on a never ending line of twine.
"Hey – get out of the way." he shouted, making them jump. There was the red brick wall! Crashing to a halt he flung down the bike and peeped over the wall. There she was, asleep in a chair, under the araliya tree, her book fallen on her lap. The golden fluff lay snoring beside her. Wish I could be golden fluff, he sighed, as he threw the note with careful aim. It landed by the book on her lap. Ah – perfect. He smiled to himself and rode away.

A dark cloud wandered slowly, towards the red and blue kite, moving like a great ball of smoke saturated to bursting point. When it would burst, was its own secret. No one would know, and it would burst just like that – whenever it wanted to. It passed over the school and the clock tower and the playing field. Then houses, dozen of them cluttered together, like a pile of boxes. Then more houses set in large gardens. Suddenly the cloud bumped into a red and blue kite, bouncing right over it and making

110

it wobble and flutter towards the ground. The two boys yelled. The cloud lowered itself slightly. The araliya tree stood firm, its white flowers waving in the breeze. Through the branches the fading sun cast its pale rays touching a young girl who lay on a chair fast asleep, her book fallen by her on the grass, a flower caught in between her still fingers. The golden light glinted on the dog, lying on her back nearby, paws up in the air, fast asleep, sending out little grunts from time to time.

The cloud could hold itself no longer. It expanded and a tiny little rupture appeared at the bottom. The first drops caught the kite and it shuddered and plummeted helplessly. The boys tugged and twisted at the string, running about and shouting. Now the drops fell in a curtain making the boys grab their kite. Holding it over their heads they dashed for cover.

Voices screeched.
"It's raining – take the clothes inside."
"I thought you wanted them put out in the back garden-"
"It's going to rain you fool – take them in – quick-"

Ginger and white was snoozing peacefully when the blobs of water pelted him. He jumped to his feet, shook himself, darted onto the roof, and scrambled towards his hiding place under the eaves. The crows on the araliya tree stopped in mid squabble, dropped the fish bone and took off with a mighty flutter. The rain fell rapidly now, turning the leaves of the araliya wet and glossy. The white flowers nodded as the tree held up its arms to soak in the water. Rain filtered through the branches, in between the leaves and fell onto the sleeping Anushka and her dog. The golden spaniel sprang up, barked and scampered away.

Anushka awoke with a start.

"Oh! It's raining!" she cried. Clutching her book, she grabbed her chair and dashed into the house. She never noticed the folded note, which slid down from her lap and sank into the wet grass. In a few seconds the paper grew soggy and the words on it vanished in a blur.

Freedom Bound

His name was Francis. Some people called him Prancis, or Pranci. Never sure of what his age was – Francis was sometimes fifty, sometimes sixty four, sometimes even seventy. He was small-made, nut brown and scrawny, and looked like a dried up coconut. A few straggly hairs lay across his head and a rough stubble covered his face. As he lay huddled on the pavement he felt a prod in his ribs. He stirred but didn't get up. Then a voice. The Inspector's voice he knew so well now.

"Ah – get up get up –" the prod was harder and hurt.

He sat up. The Inspector was walking around with some policemen, waking up all the vagrants and beggars who were sleeping underneath the shop awnings.

"Important visitor coming today to Colombo – Bulgarian Prime Minister – can't let him see beggars on the roads no. Come, come – hurry up -get into the van".

Francis gathered the dirty torn sheet which he used to cover himself and walked to the blue van. It was already almost full. He squeezed himself into a corner at the edge. When they shut the doors he could hardly breathe, but better to be at the edge than in the middle inhaling each other's stink. They bumped along the pot-holed roads and after a while he saw, through the tiny grill at the top of the door, the walls of the prison where they would spend the next few weeks.

Even the cells were crowded. Back again, Francis thought, greeting old friends like Thatte Sunil and Kalu Siri. The last time he was here he had the 'flu' and wanted to stay in for a few extra days, but no - they just threw him back onto the streets. Later a snippet captioned a picture on the front page of the Weekend News "Meliwada Prison releases fifty of its inmates on the death anniversary of our late Prime Minister." The picture showed several men and women walking out of the high gates of the prison, carrying little bundles tucked under their arms. The print was too small to detect their expressions. There was always some occasion to throw them in and another to throw them out.

Outside, the sun blinded him, especially after being used to the dismal cell. Of course there was their exercise time or some manual work to be done, but the glimpse of the outside was never for too long. Francis had no personal belongings other than his cover-sheet. He folded it into a tiny rectangle and tucked it inside his shirt so his hands were free. Once outside, he dug out a beedi from his shirt pocket – the last of ten which he managed to get from the Prison Guard in exchange for the ten rupees he had on him at the time he was picked up. Lighting it he inhaled savouring its pungent flavour. Now he was at the main road – the newly built highway. He stood on the pavement smoking his beedi and watched the vehicles zooming past as if driven by demented drivers. His stomach rumbled reminding him of the morning meal he had missed. For though the stringhoppers were always dry, and the sprinkling of sprats could hardly be found in the thin gravy, still it filled his stomach. *The mean buggers released us without giving us any breakfast even - ah well, I'll go to the Missi's house – I can get something to eat there, and I'm sure she'll give me some money also.*

As he didn't have money even for bus fare, he resigned himself to the long walk he would have to make to Kirullaponne where the Missi lived. This is where he had worked twice a week for almost ten years. The Missi never turned him away, except when he went there after liquor.

Then her face would become like a jambu, her eyes would bulge out of their sockets and she would scold him in a loud voice. But a week later he would go there, and she'd ignore him for a while but later she would tell Somalatha to give him something to eat.

The sun blazed and Francis rested on the pavement under a large tree. *By now we would be having our mid morning tea, plain -but I always got two spoons of sugar.* It was hot under the tree too, but he was out of the sun's dazzling rays. Crows swooped down near him to dig into a chunk of bread someone had thrown on the road. They attacked it with their beaks, each trying to get the biggest piece. People passed, most of them on their way to work or to school. Rushing, rushing like life itself was going to stall on them. Thank goodness I don't have to hurry like that, he thought. Two stray dogs, one with a chewed up ear and the other with a limp, came along and sniffed around him but decided that the garbage scattered nearby was more interesting. Francis must have sat there for about half an hour when suddenly luck struck him in the form a ten rupee note thrown to him by a passerby who mistook him for a beggar! Chuckling, he climbed the footboard of a crowded bus and gripped the handrail as they jerked forward.

Soon he was at the new green gate the Missi had installed only last year. When the dogs saw him they greeted him with barks and howls. Somalatha the old woman who worked there came out.

"Ah Pranci Aiya! – where have you been?"

"In the *hira gedera* – don't you know – usual thing." He grinned showing broken discoloured teeth.

"All this time – now nearly three weeks you didn't come no?"

"Yes –that's the thing, we were taken before that Bulgarian Prime Minister came and released today because it's our former Prime Minister's birthday.

Somalatha opened her eyes wide, flummoxed that there were so many Prime Ministers in this world. "Ah really! Missi was waiting for you last week also."

Mrs Goonewardena came out at the sound of Francis's voice.

"Ah Francis- where on earth have you been?"

When he told her she sighed. "Aiyo what a sin no – to put you in prison just to keep the place looking spic and span for the Bulgarian man. They always do this just to impress the visitors." She paused. "Somalatha give him something to eat. Francis you can have a bath here."

Somalatha went inside to serve him some food.

"What a crime to put these people away like this and then throw them out when they feel like it! Poor chap!"

Francis bathed and changed into the same dirty shirt and sarong.

Mrs Goonewardene came out with an old shirt and sarong of her husband's and gave it to him. "Here, you can take these and keep this fifty rupees also."

"When can I come and work here Missi?"

"Come next week – I already had to get someone else to do your work this week. I didn't know what had happened to you. Anyway come next Wednesday."

Francis wore the 'new' clothes and sat down to eat. Somalatha was mixing the dogs' food at the table in the garden.

"Why are you sleeping on the pavement? You must find a good place to stay. When you sleep on the pavement the police will always be catching you and putting you in prison."

"That's the thing- but what to do?" He paused. "Maybe I'll ask the Missi to get me a job."
"Some place where you can stay no? That's the best thing."
"Very difficult to get that kind of a job."
"Anyway, ask the Missi – she knows lots of people, she'll be able to help you."

When Mrs Goonewardena returned he said, "Aiyo Missi, can you find me a job- somewhere where I can stay?"
She thought for a while. "I'll try– can't promise, it's very difficult these days, but I'll try."

By strange coincidence that very afternoon her friend Sheila who was the Matron at the St Mary's Girls' Hostel at Nawala rang her.
"Yvette, can't you find us a caretaker for this place? We are stuck as the old fellow died last month and we still haven't been able to find someone."
Caretaker? Francis? The two words sprang into her mind.
"I'll look around," she said without wanting to commit herself.

When he arrived on the Wednesday she spoke to him about the job.
"Francis this is a good chance for you to get settled in a good place. I'll give you a letter of recommendation – don't worry. The interview is on Saturday at 10 o'clock – don't go late."
He smiled. "How to wear these old clothes for the interview Missi?"
Mrs Goonewardene rummaged through her husband's cupboard. She found another hardly used shirt and then she remembered the sarong she had bought over Christmas

for the baases – there should be one remaining out of that lot.

Francis was seated on the small stool in the garage drinking a cup of tea.

"Here Francis - some good clothes – and don't forget to bathe and shave before you go on Saturday."

He came on the Saturday morning dressed in the clothes she'd given him. His face was shining, free of the stubble that usually spotted his face. But what was that in his hand? A dirty paper bag filled with something.

"Oh Francis – you can't carry that dirty bag when you go for the interview, here let me give you something better." She went into her kitchen and brought out a clean plastic bag into which he upset the contents.

"Then I'll go Missi."

"Yes Francis – and good luck to you."

She looked at the clock and thought, Francis must be at his interview - wonder how he's doing?

Late that evening the Matron rang her. "Yvette, that man you sent was really good. He seemed to be exactly what we were looking for. So neat and clean – a very pleasant fellow. He's got the job –with that recommendation you sent he could have got the job of the Chairman no!"

"I'm so happy he's got the job."

"Yes – we've offered him two five a month, all three meals, and will give him a room with a bathroom outside. I spoke to the Chairman and can organize a fan for the room also. He will have to mop the floors and clean the place and also keep the garden tidy. He will also have to go to the kadé whenever we need something –it's just round the corner. Ah – and he spoke so much about you that we told him he could take a day off to work at your place because we didn't want him to miss out on some extra money."

118

Mrs. Goonewardena was pleased she hadn't lost him, but most of all she was happy he finally had a proper place to stay – no more being picked up and thrown into prison.

Francis didn't turn up the next day, nor the next. Mrs. Goonewardene knew he had to take up duties at his new job in a few days' time and wondered why he didn't come to tell her the good news. Four days passed before he made his appearance.

On hearing his voice she rushed outside. Beaming she said "Ah Francis – I heard you got the job – very good very good!"

He scratched his head and gave a weak smile.

"I will give you a nice plastic bag and get you some clothes and –"

"No use Missi –". He looked down.

"But you'll need these things –"

" I am not going."

" Not going?"

"Not going for the job."

"But why?"

He shifted his feet and screwed up his mouth. "Aiyo Missi – the salary is not enough, they will pay only two thousand five hundred – that's very little no."

"But that's better than nothing – also they will give you three meals and a day off to work here."

"That's true, but anyway how can I be cleaning the house and the garden every single day – too much of work no– I have to go to the kadé also and mop the place and cut the grass and all that."

"But you won't have to cut the grass every day? Surely!"

He rattled on, "Also they told me that I must come in by 9.30 every night as the place had to be locked up at that time. Big nuisance no, to come in at that time every single

119

night. Then I don't have any freedom to do what I want.
What if I want to stay out late? So much work and not a big
salary even and then I have to come in early also."
"But you'll have a place to stay and a bathroom and –"
"But not enough salary, and too much work. And my
freedom – that's also cut. So I don't like to take the job."
Mrs. Goonewardena was still and silent. Then she spoke,
her voice subdued. "Okay then – so you don't want the job.
You must go immediately and tell that Matron Missi that
you are not taking it. Go now and tell her."
"I thought Missi can phone and tell–"
"No –*I am* not telling them – yo*u* tell them."
She went inside shutting the door firmly behind her.
Somalatha was witness to all this and knew the lady was
upset. She followed her inside. "Don't worry lady – lady
tried no to get him a job, what to do if he doesn't like? Next
time mustn't try even."
There'll never be a 'next time' Mrs. Goonewardene thought
as she sat at the kitchen table.

He didn't turn up for several weeks after this. Then one
morning when the sun was burning down and dust rose up
from the gravel roadway, there he was.
The dogs ran up to the gate wagging their tails and
barking. Somalatha came out of the kitchen.
"Ah Pranci aiya where were you?"
"In the hira gedera – don't you know. Today only they let
me off." He grinned. "I was wondering whether there's
anything for me to eat – I feel quite hungry."

Acknowledgements

Many have helped me with this publication.

- Countless thanks to my husband and best friend Simon, for his incredible patience and tolerance of my eccentricities -which are many! Also for his positive comments and guidance.

- I am grateful to my children and their spouses - Sonali & Dinesh and Dimitri & Sarah - for their loyal support; my Gorgeous Grandchildren, Akash and Audrey - the sunshine and rainbows in my life.

- My helper Kusuma who gives me the time I need to do my writing;

- Emma and Lindy and other little friends around the house - my de-stressing agents.

- Immense gratitude to Christine Wilson for her friendship and constructive advice.

- Many thanks to Yasmine Gooneratne, Sita Kulatunga and Tissa Abeysekera for using precious time to read my book and for their comments on the back cover.

- The Wadiya Group and The English Writers Cooperative of Sri Lanka for publishing my work in their journals and for sharing ideas.

- My Printer Ariya and Graphics expert Charith for their expertise and patience.

- Above all, thank you God for always being there for me.